PRASE FOR T

MW00623480

"The Best Good Horse is a collection of timeless stories about people trying to do the next good thing for themselves. There is a quiet intensity in these short stories. ... the tones and moods work together to craft tales that are distinct from one another."

—CLARION REVIEW, 5-STAR REVIEW

"Lovers of literary fiction and complex characters will appreciate this collection that is as tragic as it is innocent."

—PUBLISHERS WEEKLY/BOOKLIFE

"Moody memorable tales powered by human struggle, tenacity and an unshakable sense of survival. ... grounded in the beauty and intricate complexities of the human condition."

—KIRKUS REVIEW

"The Best Good Horse and Other Short Stories is a literary collection that will appeal to readers who enjoy vignettes about ordinary peoples' extraordinary moments of their lives. ... what connects these works is a sense of place, time, and evolution that makes each story a tiny treasure of insight and revelation."

—D. DONOVAN, SENIOR BOOK REVIEWER, MIDWEST BOOK REVIEW

J. Reeder Archuleta offers a collection of 14 short stories that focus on a bevy of tough and engaging individuals dealing with life from various points of the moral spectrum. ... a subtle quiet blend of place, character, and individual story lines. ... endings are consistently thought-provoking."

—BLUE INK REVIEWS

"A satisfying collection of human triumph and courage, each story introduces readers to a new set of characters who fight, claw, and battle their way out of the mess to become a survivor."

—RABIA TANVEER FOR READERS' FAVORITE, 5-STAR REVIEW

THE BEST GOOD HORSE

THE
BEST
GOOD
HORSE

AND OTHER SHORT STORIES

J. REEDER ARCHULETA

IZZARD INK PUBLISHING
PO Box 522251
Salt Lake City, Utah 84152
www.izzardink.com

Library of Congress Cataloging-in-Publication Data
Names: Archuleta, J. Reeder, author.
Title: The best good horse : and other short stories / J. Reeder Archuleta.
Description: First edition. | Salt Lake City, Utah : Izzard Ink Publishing, [2022]
Identifiers: LCCN 2021062511 (print) | LCCN 202106 (ebook) |
ISBN 9781642280760 (hardback) | ISBN 9781642280777 (paperback) |
ISBN 9781642280784 (ebook)
Subjects:
Classification: LCC PS3601.R389 B47 2022 (print) |
LCC PS3601.R389 (ebook) | DDC 813/.6—dc23/eng/20220214
LC record available at https://lccn.loc.gov/2021062511
LC ebook record available at https://lccn.loc.gov/2021062512

Designed by Meighan Cavanaugh
Cover Design by Andrea Ho
Cover Images: shutterstock/Menno van der Haven
First Edition

Contact the author at info@izzardink.com
Hardback ISBN: 978-1-64228-076-0
Paperback ISBN: 978-1-64228-077-7
eBook ISBN: 978-1-64228-078-4

"Precious Pete's Legacy" and "The Foundling Home" appeared in
Rio Sonora, originally published in 2010 by the author.

CONTENTS

THE BEST GOOD HORSE

A PRAYER TO
SAINT MICHAEL

No one in the valley knew his name, so they simply called him Al's brother. They knew he was here to take care of his brother's ranch after Al, who had lived in the valley for ten years, died several months earlier. One rancher remembered that Al had once mentioned a brother but no one seemed to know any details about him. Al had been a respected rancher in the valley with a reputation for being friendly and could always be counted on for a round of drinks at the Cotton Club. He maintained his good humor even after his wife left him about seven years previously. After she left, Al had begun to spend more time in town away from the demands of his ranch. Then about six months ago, Al became very sick and it didn't take long for the illness to steal his strength and rob him of his mobility. Less than two weeks after his last trip to town Al died. He had left written instructions for his burial on a small hill behind the barn. The talk among his friends then turned to the grazing value of his two-section spread and the fact that there were two wells on the place and how this would make it a good place to grow alfalfa. Most of the speculation took place at the Cotton Club where all current and past business in the valley was discussed, and always over a game of dominoes.

The man they called Al's brother kept to himself, but when he was seen around town folks liked the fact that he was friendly and always polite. Mrs. Johnson, the postmistress, told her friends that she had seen him hold the post office door open for old Mrs. Egstrom on several occasions when he came in to check on his brother's mail, and he always had a kind word for her and anyone else who happened to be in the building at the time. Mrs. Johnson did not mention to her friends that she thought he was a very handsome man and that she always found a reason to try to engage him in conversation. But this did not do her much good, as he was a man of few words, almost shy, and their conversations never went beyond pleasantries.

After a while, the people in the valley accepted the fact that Al was gone and his brother would be here until he made a decision about the ranch. But the arrival of another stranger in a brand-new Ford sedan began a new round of talk. This stranger, who everyone agreed was obviously a city slicker, had been seen with Al's brother at the Lone Star. The stranger was wearing a blue blazer with brass buttons, gray wool slacks, a white shirt, and polished shoes. This was considered formal dress in the valley, and only someone from the city would appear in such clothes. So, it was decided that this man was no doubt a banker here on some kind of business having to do with Al's ranch, and there was a certain amount of concern, for none of them trusted anyone from any bank. Everyone present at the Lone Star that day had listened closely, trying to hear what the two were discussing, but were disappointed when the two men spoke only a few words to each other. After they finished their meal, the well-dressed stranger got into his Ford and drove off out of town, not even stopping for gas at the El Paso Red Flame.

Al's brother did have a name. Several in fact. The man from the city called him Adam. Adam was a code name assigned to him during the war. The man from the city had the code name Mark and neither of them ever used their true names in conversation with each other. This was normal for those who lived in the world they both were a part of. Nobody knew about the conversation between Mark and Adam that took place at Al's ranch house earlier that day.

"I wish you would reconsider, Adam. At least think it over before turning me down."

"I appreciate the fact that you came all the way out here to see me, but things have changed." Adam was not surprised that Mark had found him in this remote part of Texas. It was, after all, what they did best.

"The boss hopes that you will accept. You know that we both think highly of you. And he wanted me to tell you that most of the old outfit has been re-formed and it has a new name and mission."

"Yes. Still with three initials?"

"Actually no. Not that one. We don't have initials or even a real name because officially we do not quite exist. We will be a much smaller group than before and we have a very specific assignment, similar to our old one but more . . . well, more relevant and modern. I am happy to report that some of our old colleagues are already back on board. The boss wanted me to tell you that your compensation will be considerably more than the captain's rate you got back then. No more living rough and having to make do. Travel and accommodations will all be first class."

"I'm getting along fine."

"This?" Mark waved his arm around the main room of the ranch house.

"Maybe. Haven't made up my mind whether to sell it or keep it."

"I just cannot picture you growing corn or pigs or whatever, when there is still meaningful work to be done. Where's the old spirit, eh?" Mark had always affected a slightly British manner of speaking. Adam supposed it was due to all the time he spent in London at their old headquarters. Whatever the reason, it came across as phony and it always irritated Adam.

"I will tell you that one of our first assignments is to deal with the group responsible for what happened to Therese." Mark noticed Adam's eyes come alive as they met his and locked on for a second. "I thought that might get your attention. Tell you what, no need for an answer now. Take some time and consider it and then call me at this number. Use our old code names when you ask for me. The boss and I would be most delighted with a reply in the affirmative." He handed Adam a slip of paper. "Is there a place where we can get a bite to eat before I start back?"

Adam sat in his brother's chair on his brother's porch and watched the county road that ran north to south in front of the property. In his opinion his brother, Alain, had built the ranch house too close to the road. There were several young men who lived in a small house about a mile south who drove a new Chevrolet V-8 Coupe at high speeds up and down the road at all times of the day and night. The roar of its exhaust had woken Adam on several occasions. He had asked himself, why even have a ranch if you could not have a bit of seclusion and privacy? He would have built the house at least a half mile from the road.

He remembered the last time that he had seen Mark. It was Christmas, 1945, in a small office in a nondescript building in midtown Manhattan. It was to be the last meeting with the one they called the boss, the man who had led their team, which was a small offshoot of the newly formed Strategic Services. It was their final debriefing before he was mustered out of service. It had not been a pleasant parting. He had been obsessed with their last mission, which had failed and resulted in the abduction of Therese. It had been yet another incident of betrayal and he had expressed anger and insisted on a move against the responsible group. He had always suspected that there was too much loose talk in London and thought that the headquarters people, those Harvard and Yale amateurs that Donovan surrounded himself with, had let the details of the mission leak to impress their friends. But the war was over. The enemy had surrendered unconditionally and there was, as Mark had explained, "naught" one could do. It was not in Adam's nature to forgive and forget and it had taken some time for him to accept the inevitable. These things happened in war and it was one of the risks they had taken. The war was long over, he thought. We won. Good people died. Therese is gone. And now, no more killing, no more suspicions or betrayals, and his need to strike back was nothing but a small itch hidden deep inside.

The anger had consumed him and then slowly, very slowly, the bitterness faded as he lived in memories of Therese and their time together. In all honesty he was never sure that the bond they shared would have lasted beyond the war. They were products of two very different worlds, but together they thrived in one of chaos and intrigue. In a peaceful setting, the relationship would probably have gone to hell in a hurry but he knew he would never have anything like it again. They had lived with an intensity in a time when all pretense was stripped from daily life. It was a time that demanded clear, logical thinking along with a daring resolve. Her code name was Therese. He knew her true name but somehow could not put it together with the woman he knew and loved. Therese was passionate, committed, feared nothing, and possessed a near ruthless devotion to their mission. He suspected that the Germans had done something awful to her or a loved one to make her so dedicated to their destruction, but he did not want to know the story. They had never asked about each other's past, did not even think about discussing the future, but were happy to live out their time in a place gone mad with war.

So now, in his time of peace, he sat on the front porch of his brother's ranch house and considered his future and the details of his brother's estate. He learned from the lawyers that the property was paid off years ago and that after the medicos had told his brother of the finality of his illness, he had sold off the livestock and most of the equipment. He had then placed all his assets in a trust, named his only living relative, his brother, as co-trustee and sole beneficiary and turned over the care of the trust to his father's old law firm.

Adam watched the sun go behind the mountains to the west, and as it disappeared, the sky became a sheet of bright red. There is a calmness here, he thought, and it is beginning to cover the old scars and all the violent times. He was content that the old feelings he had held close were leaving him and he was glad to retreat into that elusive state of grace that only came when he remembered the time of Therese. He continued to watch until the outline of the mountains faded into the darkness of the night sky.

———

As was his custom, Rip O' Leary ended the night at the Cotton Club where he had picked up a little over five dollars in a domino game. He then tried to spend it all at the bar but had time for only two before closing time. He bought six more to go then got into his old pickup truck and headed home. As he passed by the picture show building, he noticed Agatha Palmer's old Hudson with a flat tire and a spindly bumper jack placed under the rear bumper. He pulled over next to the car which was in the deep shadow of the building. He could see that no one was around and concluded that Aggie caught a ride home and would come back to change the tire in the morning. He slowly drove back onto Main Street and headed out of town to his family's old homestead. After a while, he found himself driving down the well-packed county road that passed in front of poor old Al's place and he became a bit melancholy when he realized that if old Al were still alive, he would have pulled in through the gate and shared the six-pack with him. Somehow, he could not see doing that with the brother who appeared to be a cold distant version of Al. Funny how two brothers could be so different, he thought. The road kept fuzzing up in the glare of his headlights and he countered this by blinking his eyes rapidly and taking his foot off the accelerator. Time to take a leak anyway, he thought. He brought the truck to a stop, turned the key, and opened the door. Starting to cool down, he thought as he unbuttoned his pants. There was a half moon and he could see the outline of Al's ranch house. He got back into his pickup, started it, and put it into gear when he saw two figures several hundred feet down the road in front of him. He gripped the steering wheel and stared intently trying to make out who these people were. As he stared, the two figures blended into one. It was a human form, stark white on the road and walking in a jerky manner, toward him. He reached into the glove box and took out his old Colt. He was taking no chances with whoever or whatever this was. He lit a cigarette and watched as the human shape slowly made its way toward him. As it got closer, he thought that it appeared to be a naked female but did not trust his judgment because of the beer. Then as his eyes refocused, he realized that it was Aggie Palmer. Her long dark hair hung down on her shoulders and her skin was stark white in the light of the moon and the glare of his head-lights. She was walking with a bad limp. She held one arm close to her with the other one. He also noticed some dark splotches on her naked body. He got out of the pickup and called her name. He heard her sob and she sat down in the middle of the road. He caught himself staring at her nakedness and reached into the cab of his truck and took out his old field jacket. He walked over to her and placed the coat over her shoulders and that was when he noticed that the dark splotches were dried blood and what appeared to be bruises.

Aggie looked at him with a blank expression and told him in a calm voice that she needed to get home. Rip asked what happened to her but she ignored his question. She cried out as she tried to bring herself to her feet. Rip felt awkward helping her; he did not want to put his hands anywhere on her body that was not covered by his field jacket. He noticed that she was carrying one of her boots.

"Can I help?" The voice was so close behind him that it startled Rip and he almost fell as he turned to see who it was.

Rip saw Al's brother standing there as calm as could be as he took in the scene. Agatha saw him and averted her eyes in embarrassment. The man leaned over and pulled Rip's jacket tight around the girl's chest, placed his hands under her arms and legs and lifted her up in one swift movement.

"We need to get her into your truck and take her over to the house." He nodded in the direction of the ranch house. "Looks like her leg is broken. Is there a doctor in town?"

Rip, suddenly very sober, told Al's brother, "Her name is Agatha Palmer. There is no doctor. The nearest medical help is in El Paso."

"Right." He spoke softly to Agatha, "I am going to put you into the front seat with your legs straight out on the seat and this gentleman will drive you very carefully over to my place, that is, my brother's place. OK?" She just stared straight ahead. Rip started up the truck and drove very slowly down the road to Al's ranch house, with Adam standing on the running board.

They put Agatha on the couch in the living room and Adam went into the bedroom, returned with a blanket, and handed it to the girl. He gently removed her boot from her grip and then she wrapped the blanket around her exposed body, leaned back, and closed her eyes. Adam placed the boot on an old roll-top desk next to the bookcases.

"Agatha, what I would like to do is patch up what we can and then get you to some real medical care. Please do not be embarrassed. I am only trying to help. Is that all right?" Rip noticed that he spoke quietly and he thought he noticed Aggie relax a bit.

It took ten minutes and in that time, Adam determined that she had a possible concussion, a broken nose, a fractured tibia, and possible fracture of the right ulna. There were also contusions on other parts of her body. He noticed that there was swelling on the knuckles of both hands and her short fingernails were broken. He dressed the cuts and abrasions with iodine and decided against trying to set the fractured tibia. If they hurried, she would be in a hospital in El Paso within a couple of hours. As he was calculating the time and the care needed, he felt the old desire for vengeance push into his thoughts, because he knew her injuries were not a result of a car crash or any other accident. He knew without looking that she had been raped. The beating that she took was administered by a sadist. Of that he had no doubt. It was obvious that she had fought back and as a result had suffered some defensive wounds. This girl had courage, he thought, and if there were no serious internal injuries, she would survive. But she would carry scars. The physical ones would heal fastest and it would be up to her to heal the others as well as she could. He had done all he could and now it was time to get her to a hospital. He took the bandages and medicine back into the kitchen. Rip followed him.

"I know what happened and who did it!" he said in a low voice.

Adam turned to look and him and saw an angry determined face.

"Who would do such a thing?" Adam asked in a disinterested voice.

"The Hazen boys, down the road."

"Those guys with the V-8 Chevy?"

"That's them and by God I will square things away!" Rip was clenching his fists. The effects of the alcohol had worn off and he was ready for a fight.

"No, my friend. This is a matter for the law."

"The law? You and I both know how that will end up."

Adam shrugged. "I want to help but I don't want to get involved. This is a matter for the authorities. Right now, we need to get her some serious medical help. Where will you take her in El Paso?"

"County hospital. Aggie's family ain't exactly well off."

"Do you know where Hotel Dieu is? Up on Stanton?"

"Yeah. But Aggie ain't a Catholic and like I told you, she doesn't have much money."

"Wait one minute." Adam turned and went down the hall to the bedroom.

He came back with an envelope and some writing paper. He sat down at the kitchen table and wrote out a short paragraph on the paper. He folded the paper over six fifty-dollar bills and placed them in the envelope. He then wrote a name on the envelope, sealed it, and handed it to Rip. He also handed him another fifty-dollar bill.

"Take Agatha to Hotel Dieu Hospital. Ask for Sister Marie Claire. She is a nun and a nurse. Give her this envelope and use the other money for gas and lodging if you have to stay in El Paso overnight. I will have to ask you to please not mention this to Agatha or anybody else. Remember, ask only for Sister Marie Claire and hand her this note. Will you do that?"

"I will!" Rip said. He thought that maybe this guy was every bit as good as Al and that made him certain that his generosity would be their little secret.

"You will also need to notify the authorities. I will remain here. Tell the sheriff I will be here and can provide testimony as a witness."

"OK, but you be careful should them two come looking for her."

"I'll lock up and stay right here. I don't believe they'll come over and cause trouble, will they?"

"You don't know them two bastards! Just be careful!"

"I will. Now let's get Agatha out to your truck."

Adam stood near the gate and watched the lights of Rip's pickup fade on the road into town. He had become the Adam of old. The instincts, the cold, analytical thinking, and the plans for action took over in a heartbeat. He asked himself why. This has nothing to do with you. The girl is nothing to you, he thought. Your thinking is from a different time. A time when there was something to fight for. An enemy to destroy. You don't know this girl. Leave it! It has nothing to do with you! But he knew that he had already lost the fight, because he knew that her faith in others was gone forever. It was always gone when the bastards did what they did. But he knew he really had lost the fight when he saw her eyes while she was down on the road, holding tight onto a scuffed boot as if that would keep her in the world that she had woken up to this morning and not in the world of the animals that gave her pain. It was the eyes. They always told you that the world had changed forever. No more smiles, no more pleasant small talk. The joy and plans for the good life with someone gone forever. He had seen it during the war. The picture of life with a Robert or Pierre or Dieter, or whoever, was flamed out into ashes of bitterness and a fear that would live with her the rest of her life. And despite all the years that had passed since he had last seen that look, he now stood there as if it were only yesterday.

He looked down the empty road to town for a while longer and then turned and went inside. He calculated that he had roughly one hour at the most. He went into the bedroom and removed a Colt Model 1917 revolver from the nightstand. He thumbed the cylinder release and pushed the cylinder out of the frame. He studied the primers on the cartridges and the half-moon clips holding them in place, then he closed the weapon and replaced it in the drawer. No, he thought, no evidence trail. And then in the darkest, most remote part of him, the thought began to stir that the old revolver would not satisfy his need.

He went out to his brother's wood shop and turned on the light. He looked around and quickly spotted a short ten-inch wooden dowel. That'll do, he thought. He hit the light switch on his way out of the house. There was a rough dirt road that ran south past the old barn. It was parallel to the county road and was a good one hundred yards inside the fence line of his brother's property. He began a slow, steady jog south in the direction of the Hazen brothers' house. In less than ten minutes he could see the lights of their place. He sat down in the dirt road, pulled off his boots and placed them next to a creosote bush. He then made his way, in stocking feet, to the fence line and the county road.

The door to the house was unlocked and he carefully pushed it open. The lights were on and he saw that the brothers were asleep, the larger of the two on a sofa and the smaller one in a chair. There was a heavy nine-millimeter auto, a Browning High Power, on the table next to the chair. He looked to make sure the small thumb safety was engaged. His eyes searched the room and found a pair of jeans and some women's underwear in a crumpled heap next to an end table. Then he saw one Western style boot with a scuffed toe next to the pile of clothing. He moved quickly to the clothing and picked up the boot. Without touching it, he put the High Power in the boot and felt it slide down to the heel. He gauged the distance between himself and the two men. The one in the chair was closest so he edged over to him. He grabbed the boot by the top and swung it in a short powerful arc so the heel, with the weight of the pistol inside, struck the smaller one on the side of his head. He put the dowel in his back pocket. There was no need for it.

———————

He drove north on Stanton Street and could see the outline of the six-story building at the corner of Arizona Street. He pulled into the parking lot on Stanton across from the hospital. He remembered the old Hotel Dieu further down Stanton; as a young boy, he had always thought of the old brownstone building as one of those spooky places that housed old witches and ghosts. The new hospital was clean and bright and the pride of the Daughters of Charity. He went to the front desk and asked for Sister Marie Claire. He waited for her at the edge of the reception area where the afternoon sun slanted through the blinds. From the corner of his eye, he saw Marie Claire, as beautiful as ever, walk, with her confident stride, into the room. Smiling, she grabbed both his hands in a firm grasp and they both stood quietly. It had been a long while and they were remembering each other in another time.

"Gerard, mon cher, you are well?" She spoke French in a soft voice.

"Yes, I am well. And you?" He answered in the same language, using the familiar form.

She glanced quickly at the receptionist who was talking on the telephone. "Let's go to my office." She turned and led him to a door marked "Director of Services."

They sat in silence for a while, smiling at each other.

"You are here to see the girl?"

"No. I do not want to cause her any embarrassment."

"Gerard makes another good decision, no? She is indeed a very proud young woman and at this moment very injured. But she is in good hands. Of course, I did not mention your note or the money."

"Thanks."

"Mon cher! You almost blushed." She gave him a mischievous grin. "You know her well?"

"No. Only from when she was found."

"And les affreux who did this to her?" Marie Claire's eyes grew hard and she frowned.

He avoided her eyes. He did not want to lie to her.

"Oh," she said, "I think I know it now!" She was quiet for a moment. An old-fashioned alarm clock on a bookcase ticked away the seconds. Then Marie Claire spoke as if addressing a third person in the room. "And you will cast into hell all the evil spirits who wander through the world seeking ruin of souls."

"I did not say—"

She held up her hand. "It is only a prayer to Saint Michael. It has always reminded me of you, not the Gerard, but the Adam, and of the time we spent looking for evil men who were given free rein by an even more evil one. But les affreux who did this to the girl called Agatha? They answer only to themselves. When I saw her, I knew that I had become too comfortable in believing that the evil was behind me. But at least I know that whoever did this will not do it again. I am glad that you have not changed."

He shook his head and grinned. "The question is: have you?"

"After the war I was looking to leave that time behind me and start over. And you told me about this place here in this far corner of Texas and the world. I envisioned a place filled with bawdy saloons and gunfighters and cowboys. Of course, it was nothing like that and it has helped me. The men from your father's firm were so discreet and helpful. But there are times . . . ." She became quiet and then after a while she said, "An old friend came around to visit me the other day. He made me quite an offer. Please, Gerard, you don't need to tell me about his visit with you. I think I know the answer."

He held her gaze. "He would expect you to renounce your vows."

"In my order, we renew our vows every year and I am free to walk away once every twelve months."

He willed himself to not say another word and made every effort to keep a poker face. They were getting too near to something that was so closely held by each of them. Neither of them nor even other members of their old team would dare think about disclosing their feelings about such an offer made by the one called Mark. Marie Claire slowly got up and held the door to her office open. They were comfortable in each other's company.

They walked out of the hospital together and made small talk about the weather and the traffic. They talked about anything but what was on their mind. They did not say goodbye. He nodded to her in a formal manner and she smiled as she watched him walk across the street. And then she admitted something to herself that she would never tell him. She had always envied their friend, Therese, who had the love of this man when he was called Adam.

———————

The building that housed the Texas Department of Public Safety sat next to an empty lot just off the main highway that ran from El Paso to San Antonio. At the back of the building an office with its own entrance housed the Texas Rangers of Company E. Normally there were two Rangers assigned to investigate serious crimes in the westernmost territory of the state, but for the past month there had been only one; the other had retired and had not yet been replaced.

It was a small office with a prison-made wooden desk and three chairs. There was a metal filing cabinet along one wall with a hat rack above it. The opposite wall held the portraits of Rangers killed in the line of duty. The Spartan nature of the office was not because the State of Texas was miserly in meeting the needs of the Ranger force. In fact, the Rangers were provided with the most modern equipment available. But the Rangers had always believed that investigations were to be conducted face-to-face and that crimes were solved in the field, not in a cozy office with its own coffee machine. Rangers were expected to spend their days in the field whether it was in an off-road vehicle or horseback. This philosophy suited the type that made up the force. Every Ranger had long experience in law enforcement before being selected to the force and they all preferred to be out in the open space of Texas than behind a desk in a cramped office.

Ranger James Castle Bruce was no different. And on this day, he was frustrated on two counts. The first was that he would rather be outside in the cool, crisp air of winter in far west Texas and secondly, he was finishing up a report on an unsolved case. The report that lay on his desk was made up of several parts: the initial incident report from the sheriff's office, his own interview of the victim and witnesses, the crime scene report, and the coroner's report. There was nothing to add nor was there any additional investigation to be conducted. He had just returned from the prosecutor's office and they had agreed that since there was no suspect or enough probable cause to name one, not to mention a lack of physical evidence, the case could not move forward. In the absence of new information that would provide for a motive and a suspect, the case could not be presented to a grand jury. It would be kept open, but with no immediate leads to cover, the Ranger could move on to other cases.

The Ranger reached for the ash tray on top of the desk and pushed around the cold cigarette butts, finally picking the largest one. He put it between his lips and struck a match. It was the last of six smokes he allowed himself each day. During his last physical exam the doctor had found a slight heart murmur along with elevated blood pressure, so he had advised the Ranger to cut down on his caffeine intake, limit fried foods—that is, broil, not fry his steaks—and to stop smoking. He had followed all but the smoking advice. He had compromised by limiting his smokes to six a day. As he sucked in the smoke from the last cigarette of the day, he realized that it was not yet noon. The nicotine calmed his frustration as he slowly reviewed the case before him.

The initial victim, a female, had been raped and viciously beaten. She had identified two brothers as her attackers. There were no witnesses to the act other than the victim and the brothers. Two after-the-fact witnesses had described what they observed when the victim was found on the road near the residence of the brothers. The medical report from the hospital provided a clinical detail of the victim's injuries and it was as bad as the Ranger had ever seen. The victim was found between one and two in the morning and arrived at Hotel Dieu Hospital at five o'clock. The sheriff and his deputy, after hearing statements from the victim and one of the witnesses, went to the brothers' residence. They had found the victim's clothing in the residence along with the two brothers. The brothers were dead, apparently murdered. The crime scene investigation conducted later that day by the Ranger and the sheriff determined that clothing found in the room with the deceased brothers did, in fact, belong to the victim. The room was filthy and disorderly but there was no sign of a struggle and no evidence that anyone had been present in that room besides the victim and the brothers. Ranger J.C. Bruce was one of the best trackers in Texas, yet he was unable to find any sign of the killer in or around the house. He found what he thought were two imprints of stockinged feet that did not fit either of the brothers, but they were faint and of no value as evidence.

The coroner found that the brothers were killed by force. The younger of the two had a blunt force wound to his right temple. His neck was also broken, the spinal cord severed at the second vertebrae. The older brother had died of suffocation because of a crushed larynx. The only other marks on their bodies were those inflicted by the victim as she attempted to fight off their attack.

The Ranger unconsciously patted his shirt pocket for a pack of cigarettes and found it empty. He looked into the ashtray for another decent-sized butt. There were none. The doctor had told him that it was merely mind over matter and that he should just form an image in his mind of himself without a cigarette. He tried very hard to do that but found himself in front of the cigarette machine in the lobby, dropping coins in the slot and listening as they rolled down the metal track, opening various gates, then pulling the knob under his favorite brand and picking the deck of smokes out of the metal tray.

As the ash formed on the fresh cigarette, he recalled the statements of the two men who had picked up the victim and treated her after the attack. They had told him nothing that would make either of them an obvious suspect in the killing of the brothers. One of the witnesses, O'Leary, was eliminated as a suspect since he had transported the victim to El Paso and remained there until noon the next day. The brothers had been killed sometime after the rape, which according to the victim, took place around midnight. Their bodies were discovered at around eight that morning.

It was way the brothers were killed that interested the Ranger. He had investigated his share of homicides and serious assaults and was familiar with violent death. But this was different. The brothers had been killed quickly and efficiently. There were men in the valley who were capable of killing. Men who had seen combat in World War II and Korea. Men who had killed before. But this one had been different and he had never seen one like it. There was no messy crime scene and there was a complete absence of physical evidence. It was more like an assassination. He had asked the coroner about the head wound on the younger one. Had it been a fatal blow? The coroner shook his head. The cause of death was the broken neck and was most likely inflicted after the blow to the temple.

The Ranger knew that whoever killed the brothers had killed like this before. It was too clean. Too quick. The killer had gone there with the killing of the brothers as his main purpose. But who could that be? The brothers had a reputation as a couple of troublemakers and there were many in the valley who, no doubt, would happily give them a good ass kicking. But murder? Where was the motive? The victim had one, and perhaps one of her kin. But the news of the assault was not even known until late in the morning, after the brothers had been killed. The only logical suspect was the one witness everyone referred to as "Al's brother." He had clear knowledge of the crime, had seen the victim, and was in the vicinity during the time frame that the murders were committed. His name was Gerard Thierry and he was residing at his deceased brother's place in order to settle his brother's affairs. He had never lived in the valley and did not even know anyone there. The Ranger's investigation showed that both Alain and Gerard were the sons of a successful and prominent lawyer in El Paso, who had died several years ago.

Then there was the fact that the female victim was taken to Hotel Dieu Hospital and not the county hospital, and her hospital bill was paid in full. The man who transported the victim claimed to have gotten lost in El Paso and found himself on Stanton Street in front of the new hospital. That was possible, the Ranger thought. But the nun in charge of operations told him that the victim was admitted as an emergency and due to the circumstances of her case, the hospital would absorb the costs of all treatment to the victim. Was the nun covering for someone? That would be hard to prove. The Ranger's investigation had revealed that the Thierry law firm had a long relationship with Hotel Dieu and that added to his suspicion of Gerard Thierry. He learned that Gerard had served in the army during World War II and the Ranger had hoped to find some background information that would support his instinct that Gerard was in fact the killer. He had found, instead, that the man had served on the headquarters staff of a logistics command in England and had never been assigned to a combat unit. He would welcome the opportunity to talk with Gerard Thierry again, but he had already interviewed him twice, the sheriff had interviewed him, and Thierry had voluntarily appeared at the prosecutor's office without a lawyer to provide yet another statement. There was absolutely no connection between Thierry and the victim. Until the time she was found, he had never even met her, so there was no logical reason to recontact him. All that remained was for the Ranger to finish the report and move on to the stack of other cases sitting in his in-box.

While the Ranger was completing his report, Gerard Thierry was conferring with one of the partners at his father's old law firm in the Mills building in downtown El Paso. He instructed the lawyer to sell the ranch and all the remaining equipment and deposit the proceeds into his account. The law firm would continue to manage Thierry's estate and serve as his point of contact.

After the meeting, Thierry left the building and walked over to Union Station. He made his way past the wooden benches to a bank of pay telephones. He reached into his pocket and pulled out a handful of coins, set them on the metal ledge beneath the telephone, inserted a dime and dialed the long-distance operator. After giving her the number he had memorized, she told him how much to deposit. He counted out the various coins and put them in the slot.

"Atlantic Trading Limited," a female voice answered.

"I would like to speak with Mark," he told her.

"One moment, please." She put him on hold and he waited a full minute.

"This is Mark."

"This is Adam. Is the job still open?"

A VERY GOOD
QUESTION

Samuel very carefully opened the door to his brother's room. The heavy wooden door swung quietly on its hinges. The room was dimly lit, the window blinds filtering the light. His brother sat up in bed, his back against the headboard. He was awake and in his left hand he held a half empty bottle of whiskey. He wore an old gray sweatshirt, thinned by age and sagging at the shoulders where, years ago, the muscled bulk of his arms had filled the cloth near to bursting.

"Come in Samuel." His brother spoke in a soft voice. He was calm; his face held a slight look of amusement.

"You OK?"

"I'm fine, Samuel." He continued in his soft voice. He was looking around the room. His head stopping occasionally, making eye contact with the people who were gathered around his bed. Samuel noticed that his eyes were red and that the bags under them seemed to grow heavier every day. His brother narrowed his eyes so that only a slit was visible. He then took a drink from the bottle.

"You're going at it kinda early, aren't you?"

"What? Oh. Just a little to get me back to sleep. I got the day watch tomorrow." He pointed around the room. "They don't care for me drinking during their visit and usually leave after I have a few."

Samuel looked around the room. Long ago he had decided that it was best to humor his brother. At one time he had thought about confronting his brother but had become afraid of what it would do to him. Samuel knew they were alone in the room but his brother knew better and it had become his reality.

"It's funny," Samuel's brother said in his low voice, "The kids always stand over there and the adults always stand there."

"When did they get here?" Samuel asked.

"I don't know. When I woke up, they were here again. They always come when they please, without me inviting them."

"What do they want this time?"

"Same as always. They want me to answer the question."

"Same question?"

"Uh-huh. They never really ask it but you can see the question in their eyes. Especially the kids." His brother looked out over the foot of his bed. There was no anger or fear in his voice.

"And what is that question?" Samuel knew that if he talked with him it helped his brother through these sessions that he called the "visitations."

"Well, it's the same question they always ask: Will you find them? I have heard that question hundreds of times. Can you find them? And some of the fellas always tell them that yes, we will. Oh, you bet, we'll find them. We always find them. Now, I wouldn't worry. Sooner or later we will find them."

"And when you tell them this, do they go away?"

"Oh, I think they would go if I told them that. But I never do, because we don't always find them. If I told them that we always find them, then I would be lying to them."

"But if you told them, then they would go away, right?" Samuel kept his voice low.

"Maybe. But they'd be back. Because they know the difference between the truth and a lie. You can't lie to them. You should never lie to them. All they really want is the truth." His brother took another drink from the bottle and Samuel saw that he was beginning to relax. His brother leaned his head against the headboard and began a small smile.

"See, Samuel. They're leaving now. I really don't think they like the whiskey."

"Well, now that they're gone, I'll let you get some sleep."

"Thanks, Samuel. Are Cath and the boys still asleep?"

"Yep, they're still asleep." Samuel lied. It was a few minutes after noon. He stood there a moment with his back against the bedroom door until his brother closed his eyes and began to snore softly. Then he went over and gently took the bottle from his hand. He put it on the night stand next to the holstered pistol. He noticed the deep creases in the black leather that snapped over the pistol's back strap under the hammer. His brother's wife bought the holster for him as a present when he was promoted to sergeant. I'll take the gun, he thought. Can't be too careful. When he reached over and picked up the gun, another, smaller piece of leather that had been leaning against the holster fell away. It was his brother's old badge holder with a metal clip on the back that would slip on to the belt in front of the holstered weapon. It looked a bit forlorn without the badge. They had taken that away from his brother a long time ago.

PRECIOUS PETE'S LEGACY

Jones and the new recruit named Ashley turned left onto Congress Street and walked over to the Palace Saloon. Jones asked after Janie Shaw and the bartender directed them to a boarding house on Second Street across the railroad tracks.

Several women lounged in the shade of the covered front porch of the boarding house and watched the men come up the front walk. They looked at the younger one with some interest but watched the older, hard-looking lawman's approach with suspicion. Jones introduced himself and his partner as Arizona Rangers and asked after Janie Shaw and her child, telling them he had a message for Janie. The oldest of the women met the Rangers at the top of the steps and had been prepared to give them a hard time but she fought hard to maintain her distrust as the older man spoke to her softly and respectfully. She sent one of the younger women into the house to find Janie and then invited the Rangers in for a drink. Jones politely apologized, saying they had to catch a train and just had time to do this favor for Janie's friend before they had to leave. The older woman and Jones were in the middle of a pleasant exchange about the weather when a plump blond with defeated eyes stepped out onto the porch.

"Miss Shaw?" Jones took off his hat.

"Yes?" Janie's eyes moved back and forth between the Rangers.

"I have a message for you from Samuel Peterson."

"Who?" she asked.

"You might know him as Precious Pete."

"Oh, him! What does that no-good sonofabitch want?" Janie stared openly at Ashley.

"He asked me to bring something to you and his daughter, Sara."

"Sara?" She took her eyes off Ashley and looked at Jones. "Sara's not his daughter! I told him that a hunnert times!"

The other girls on the porch put their hands to their mouths, trying to cover their giggles.

"He asked me to give Sara this." He handed Janie a gold piece and a ring.

"That sonofabitch! I knew it was him stole my ring. This was give to me by a fine gentleman, and I ain't seen it since the last time I seen Precious Pete!"

There was a moment of silence and the Ranger let it go on a bit before asking, in a soft voice, "And Sara?"

Janie turned to one of the younger girls. "Bonita, would you go fetch Sara." She turned back to the Ranger. "Pete always claimed Sara was his, but she ain't and that's the truth of it!" She held tightly to the ring and gold coin.

Bonita came out onto the porch holding a small, towheaded little girl. The child looked at the Rangers and then shyly buried her face in Bonita's shoulder. Just before the girl turned her head, Jones noticed crossed blue eyes and a large growth under her right ear.

"Well, I'm sure he wanted her to have it just the same, and I did promise him I'd bring it. Ladies, it's been a genuine pleasure." He reached out and gently took the madam's hand, smiled at her, and then turned and walked down the steps to the sidewalk.

Janie got up from her chair and called after the Rangers. "Where is Pete? Not that I give a damn, mind you!"

Jones stopped and looked back at Janie. "He's in Yuma prison."

"How long they keepin' him?" Janie had placed the ring on her finger and was fondling the gold piece.

"Not long. They're going to hang him for killing two ranch hands."

The madam smiled tightly and, liking the Ranger's style, watched him and the younger one walk down the street in the direction of the train station.

ACE

Winter slipped into the valley, permitting only a small blanket of warmth during the day and bringing a steady chill from sundown to sunup. Winter also brought with it the end of the farms' growing cycle. The truck crops had been gathered even before true autumn had set in; the cotton crop followed, and just before the hard frost, the last cutting of alfalfa was made. And now that alfalfa crop lay in windrows—long green lines in hard dry fields, the last signs of the valley's annual bounty.

Wiley Shaw, who had been called Ace since his high school days, slowed his brand new 1961 Cadillac to twenty miles per hour just south of the cotton gins and, right hand draped over the top of the steering wheel, began a slow cruise down the main street of town.

The Red Flame gas station came up on his left and he noticed trucks on the two hydraulic lifts, with other vehicles and pieces of farm machinery parked around the building. Business must be good, he thought. He passed by the John Deere dealership where several farmers followed the new Cadillac with their eyes as it slowly made its way to the center of town. He could see that the International Harvester shop was still in business and the drugstore parking lot was full. Everything looked the same as it did when he left seven years ago.

As he passed by his old restaurant, the Lone Star Café, Etienne, the deputy sheriff, was talking to some of the lunch crowd in the shade of the café's porch. He did not know if the deputy recognized him at this distance, and even though Ace had good memories of the deputy, he wanted to avoid him.

The valley and this small town had been his home at two different times in his life. When he was young, his father had a small ranch in the north valley and it was where Ace was raised. He hated the ranch and almost everything about it. As soon as he could he left for the oil fields of eastern New Mexico and the Permian Basin in Texas. He had worked these fields for three years and saved his money because he was a young man with a plan. The one thing he liked about the ranch was working with horses. He was good with horses. He had worked with a few, developing them into good cutting horses, but the first time he saw a quarter horse at a racetrack, he knew what he wanted to do. From that point on, he realized that he would never be happy until he owned at least one good quarter horse. When he had saved enough, he quit the oil fields, bringing his money and a girl named Pearl back to the valley. He used his savings to make a down payment on the Lone Star Café. His plan was to have Pearl run the café while he started a horse farm on some land his family had bought years ago. His father had paid off the mortgage and since Ace was his only son, he left everything to him in his will.

Ace took out a loan using his father's property as collateral and used this as seed money for his new venture, but there was more to the horse breeding business than he had ever imagined. After watching his investment drift away faster than his dreams and after the bank took back the property, he began helping Pearl try to keep the café going. After coming back to the restaurant, he'd noticed a sharp decline in the normally booming business and he learned that many of the women in town had quit patronizing the place and encouraged their friends to avoid it. Pearl claimed that they were just jealous of her good looks and pleasing personality but he had also heard rumors that she was not exactly shy about the attention she was getting from some of the local husbands. He slowly took on more duties at the café and in a short while business began to pick up again.

Then Pearl's mother became seriously ill and she had gone back to Midland to care for her during the last months of her life. During that time, he turned the business completely around and the café once again became the most popular restaurant in the county.

He made improvements to the place, buying a new stove and grill along with chairs and tables, and he improved the choices on the menu. But what made the Lone Star Café the talk of the town was the addition he had constructed out back. This building housed separate bathrooms for men and women. In the women's, he had installed two stalls and a fancy sink and kept fruity smelling bars of soap on the shelves next to the gilt framed mirror. He had placed a comfortable, small divan opposite the sink with a small footstool next to it. The bathrooms were cleaned three times a day and women raved about the cleanliness and claimed that they had never once seen a centipede or a scorpion in this fresh, clean oasis.

While he had the horse farm, he became acquainted with several people who were on the fringe of a group involved in the drug trade. They told him that he could make very easy money if he would help them hide cash from the tax man. He hesitated at first but when they revealed to him the amount of his take for this scheme, he readily agreed and was soon arranging phony purchases and sales of quarter horses. But, in spite of the additional income, the quarter horse business continued to fall apart, and it was not long before Ace admitted that it was a complete bust. After the bank took back the horse farm and his new partners knew he was broke and desperate for cash, they offered him a proposition. They explained that heroin was brought out of Mexico in stages. One group was responsible for bringing it from the interior of Mexico to the border. His new business associates took it from the border to Denver and another group distributed it from there. His friends were not a part of either the Mexico or the Denver operations. They paid the Mexicans for the dope once they took possession at the border and received payment from the other group in Denver upon delivery. They had carefully isolated themselves from both groups by being sole proprietors between receipt and delivery. His partners never let the Denver group know the details of when they picked up a load from Mexico and never told the Mexicans where the load was going. To discourage the Denver group from getting any ideas of eliminating them as middlemen they devised a system that gave them control over time and place of delivery. They brought the load to a "cooling off place" where they kept it until they established a delivery date and location. This interruption of the delivery sequence also served to screen the load's movement from the U.S. authorities. Because most shipments normally went from supplier to dealer, the routine could provide a pattern for any good investigator to follow. His partners avoided the routine and as a result, he never knew when he would be called upon to play his part, but he was always ready.

He stashed three to four kilos at a time and waited for the signal for the pickup. The heroin did not take up much space and he had constructed several hidden caches. It had worked as planned and he soon had enough money to buy back the farm if he wanted. But he had grown accustomed to the easy money and thought no more about the hard work of raising horses.

After he was paid for the last load, he never heard from his associates again. He had read every newspaper he could find to see if they had been arrested, hijacked, or murdered but he never learned a thing. Then he began to worry that the Denver group had learned of his role in the operation and he became paranoid whenever a new face walked into the café. After a year of no developments, he assured himself that for some reason the operation had simply ended and so he began to breathe easier and sleep well at night.

He had set aside twenty thousand dollars, put it into a metal box, cut up an old rubberized poncho, and wrapped the box tightly in it. He had placed the box inside the wall of the men's section of the bathroom building behind the sink vanity. He kept it there as his get-away money and never told anyone about it, not even Pearl.

After Pearl came back following the death of her mother, the café continued to be successful. And although their relationship was contentious as ever, things were going reasonably well for them until the night he shot Pearl.

That happened one evening after they had closed down the café for the day. He had never been much of a drinker but he began sipping bourbon around six that evening and by nine o'clock, he was in a nasty mood. He had learned that Pearl had taken up with one of the locals, and the fact that some farmer was sharing Pearl with him began to eat away at his pride. After an argument over her romance, at about ten o'clock on a fall evening, he pulled a snub-nose .38 out of his boot and shot her.

Pearl had been filling saltshakers at the counter near the front door when Ace pulled the trigger. The impact of the bullet knocked her onto the counter and she knocked over a pie case with four tiers of individual slices of pies on white china plates. She then slid off the Formica top and became wedged between a stool and the base of the counter. The loud report of the .38 in the café shocked Ace, and for a few minutes he just sat there, holding the revolver and smelling the burnt gunpowder as the chilled feeling of mistake slid over him in the complete silence in the room. He finally placed the revolver on the table in front of him and continued to drink from the bottle of whiskey.

He could not remember how much time had passed before he heard pounding on the front door and someone calling out his name. He sat there trying to recognize the voice when he heard Etienne's voice behind him, calm and deep.

"Ace, I want you to turn around real slow and look at me."

He turned to see the deputy holding a long-barreled revolver that looked like a child's cap gun in his huge hands. The deputy was looking across the room at the bottom of the counter where Pearl lay in a crumpled heap.

"Howdy, Etienne."

"Howdy, Ace. Is that Pearl over there?"

"Yep." His voice had no emotion.

"OK. I need you to get up and move away from the gun. Slowly now."

Ace got up and moved to the wall away from the counter. The deputy picked up Ace's revolver, moved over to the front door and opened it.

"Rip, get on in here. The rest of you wait out there until I call you."

Rip O'Leary, holding an old .45 caliber Colt pistol, limped into the café and stood two arm lengths to the deputy's left.

"Keep an eye on Ace. I'm going to check on Pearl." He knelt beside Pearl and immediately saw the wound in her right shoulder. He quickly checked her over for more damage, remembering that only one gun shot was reported. When he found no signs of other wounds, he straightened her crumpled body and moved her away from the counter.

"She's still breathing." He stood, went over to the front door, and opened it.

"Junior, you got your station wagon?"

"Right here, Etienne."

"I need you and a couple of men to take Pearl into El Paso to the hospital. She's been shot."

"You don't say, by God." Junior ran over to the vehicle, turned it around and backed it up to the front door of the café. The others brought saddle blankets and coats and lined the rear compartment of the station wagon.

Etienne shook his head. "Boys, you can take the saddle blankets out of there. Somebody grab the blankets out of my pickup and bring them over. Junior, grab some clean towels from the kitchen and put them between Pearl and the blankets." They then carefully lifted Pearl and put her in the back of the station wagon. "I'll call the state boys and warn them about you, but drive careful."

"No sweat, Etienne, we'll be at the hospital in under an hour." Junior and two others jumped into the wagon and drove off. The deputy thanked everyone for responding and told them they could go home. One of them, a young ranch hand, was looking at the spilled pie on the counter and the floor.

"Now, that's a damn shame," he said as Rip closed the door after him.

After everyone else was gone, Rip said to the deputy: "Well, not much of a mystery here, is there?"

"No. I shot her, pure and simple." Ace's voice surprised them.

"Ace, I gotta tell you that I'll have to testify to anything you tell me and it's a pure dee certainty it'll be used against you by the judge or jury."

"Don't matter. I shot her. I'm sorry about it, but I did shoot her."

"OK, Ace, I'm going to have to take you to jail and Rip is going to go with us." He reached behind him and brought out his handcuffs. "I'm going to have to put these 'esposas' on you." Etienne searched Ace for other weapons, handcuffed him and then they left for the county jail. Ace remembered walking out of the Lone Star Café into a cold, still night. The moon was well over the mountains to the east as they began the drive to the county courthouse seventy miles down the road. The rest of it had become a blur in Ace's memory. He remembered pleading guilty and telling the judge he was sorry for shooting Pearl. Pearl recovered from her wound quickly, and then immediately returned to Midland. They gave him six years and six months and sent him to Huntsville State Prison, where he later became a trusty, helping out every year at the prison rodeo. He did his time without causing any trouble and the warden recommended his sentence be reduced by six months.

The state helped find him a job in El Paso at a large warehouse down by Union Station. It was not much money, but then nobody paid people a lot of money to load and unload equipment on trucks. Eventually he reconnected with some old cronies and looked up Julio whose brother had been Ace's cell mate. Julio ran several operations dealing in stolen cars, drugs, and shylocking. Ace arranged for a loan in order to buy a new car and move into a nicer apartment. He wanted to avoid Julio's chop shop specials and found a good deal at the Cadillac dealer. He did not pay cash for the car as he told Julio he would, but made a small down payment and financed the car through the dealer. He took the rest of the cash and used it to stake a regular Thursday night poker game up near the college. It was mostly an amateur affair but he managed to double his money, and instead of paying back Julio's loan, he continued to make weekly payments on the vigorish. He found a way into a higher stakes game that a bunch of high rollers held once a week at the Paso Del Norte Hotel. Once again, his luck rode a good streak and he made more than enough to pay off both Julio and the car dealer, but instead he held onto the cash and continued to play for bigger stakes with the high rollers. He was doing well until a new player showed up. He was a young flashy dresser who put a lot of pomade in his hair and sported well-manicured finger-nails. Ace had recently gotten so confident that he had become downright cocky at the table. The new guy took all the starch out of Ace and in a two-week period steadily and thoroughly drained him of all his cash. It was done professionally and gently, with several periods of winning followed by even longer periods of losing. He was slowly lured into placing bigger bets until just like a good Ponzi scheme, it all came crashing down on him.

Word got around to Julio, who did not like the fact that Ace was obviously avoiding him and let it be known that he wanted his loan repaid in full. Julio told Ace that since he had been a good cellmate to his brother, he was giving him an extra three days to pay back the debt.

And now, as Ace sat in his new Cadillac in his old home-town, he was three days overdue. He knew he was a dead man if he didn't pay Julio, but was not worried since he was about to lay hands on his twenty-thousand-dollar stash.

Ace drove to the far end of town, pulled the Cadillac off the side of the road, and waited a while before he turned around and drove back to the café. By the time he drove into the parking lot, the deputy and the lunch crowd had left.

He sat at the counter, looked around the café, and noticed that the new owner had remodeled the place. There were new tables and chairs and the latest modern equipment behind the counter. A young waitress took his order of a T-bone steak with potatoes and coffee. He looked up as several men entered the café. He didn't know them but they nodded to him in that friendly manner that country people carry with them. He stared at the clock on the back wall but didn't even notice the time. His mind was filled with the thoughts of going out to the bathrooms and retrieving his stash. He knew he was close to solving his problem and the worries that had been with him for a week began to leave him even though his stomach still ached. The waitress brought him his order and he discovered that he had no appetite as he picked at the steak and potatoes. He felt for the screwdriver in his jacket pocket. In a while, the waitress refilled his coffee cup.

"Are the bathrooms open?" he asked.

"Oh yeah. They're out back."

"Thanks, be right back." He walked over to the side door and stepped down on the brick path he had laid out so many years ago.

He locked the door after entering the men's room and went over to the sink vanity. He noticed that the walls had been repainted a different color and the vanity was a newer model with fancy chrome fixtures, and that the old concrete floor was now covered with Saltillo tile. He opened the door under the sink where he had always kept the cleaning supplies. There was nothing in the space now except an old scrub brush and a box of soap powder. In the rear against the wall were two furring strips running vertically along the rear frame of the vanity. There were two wood screws in each strip which made it appear that the furring strips held the vanity against the wall. In fact, the screws were anchored in the wall studs and once they were backed out, the strips which were glued solidly to the sheet rock would serve as handles to pull away the cut-through sheet-rock.

He pulled the screwdriver from his pocket and in less than a minute, backed out the screws. He then pulled the sheetrock away from the wall. There it was! The old piece of rubberized poncho was still wrapped around the box. His hands shook slightly as he pulled out the box. A musty smell leaked out of the hole in the wall. He unwrapped the box and noticed that there was rust on the top of it and around the latch. He used the screwdriver to force open the lid and saw the greenbacks inside. He removed them, rewrapped the empty box, and replaced it between the wall studs. He pushed the sheetrock back in place and screwed down the wood screws, grabbed the cash, stood up, and closed the cabinet door. The pile of cash seemed smaller than when he had placed it in the metal box. He quickly counted out the bills. One thousand dollars! He slowly recounted and the amount was the same, one thousand dollars, not twenty thousand dollars! He felt light-headed and the stom-achache returned. He stood there for a moment, stunned and confused, his heart going like a trip hammer. He realized that if he stayed here any longer it would raise some questions in the café. He dropped the screwdriver behind a wall outside the kitchen door and walked back inside with the cash in his coat pocket.

He sat, sipping at his cold coffee until the waitress came over with the pot and poured a fresh cup. His mind was running at the speed limit, trying to come up with some type of plan. He needed another deal like the drug smuggling operation. Something that would make him a lot of cash quickly. The lost years in prison only reminded him that he had a lot of catching up to do.

He looked up and saw the waitress smiling at him.

"It's been a while since I've been here and I couldn't help notice that the bathroom seems different." He smiled back at the young girl.

"The owner redid most of the building last summer. Had to because of the water damage."

"Water damage?" His stomach turned over.

"Well, it seems that the swamp cooler rusted through and water flowed out and down the inside walls over a few months. Nobody noticed until the ceiling gave way and almost fell on Mr. Haggerty, who was washing his hands in the sink. So they ripped everything out and replaced it."

"I bet that was a lot of work," he said.

"The owner got the local handyman to redo the whole building."

"Who'd they get to do the work?"

"A fella they call Old Ralph. You use to live here, mister?" She looked at him like she remembered his face.

"I lived here a long time ago and I knew Old Ralph. He was a fine handyman. As I recall he was married to one of the Douglas girls."

"That's the guy, only they ain't married anymore."

He remembered Ralph the handyman. Had a deformed foot, did odd jobs around town, and was married to a very mean and disagreeable woman.

"Well, he sure did a good job. Place is good as new. Old Ralph still doin' odd jobs?"

"Maybe. But not here. He left town a week or so after he got paid for this job."

The numbness spread from his body to his brain and everything seemed to slow down. Now where would an old codger with a gimp leg go, he asked himself.

"Wonder where Old Ralph went?" he asked in a disinterested way.

"Nobody knows. He left his wife, a few hens, an old goat, and most of his tools. Nobody's heard a word since."

"Hmm." He was staring at the clock on the back wall. He noticed that it was two-thirty.

"So, do you miss this town or anybody in it?" As she smiled at him, he noticed that she wore a lot of makeup to hide the acne scars.

"What? Oh yeah, I do miss the old place." He thought about Julio and his crew and knew that he couldn't go back to El Paso. He began to sweat and the memory of the institutional smell of prison filled his nostrils. The disinfectant on the floors, the sour smell of unwashed inmates, and he could taste the watery, bland food that was slopped into the ancient, cracked plastic trays.

Most of all he remembered how time had weighed him down with nothing to break it up except the steady, measured, empty routine of a daily life, dictated by someone he had never seen. All in all, he would prefer it to returning to El Paso and facing Julio. Then he remembered that Julio and his boys could reach him in prison. Hell, they can reach out and touch me anywhere I go, he thought. He had a thousand dollars and some change, a new Cadillac whose payments were two months in arrears, and the clothes on his back. Wonder how long it'll be before the dealer reports the Caddy stolen, he wondered. Maybe I should head out across the flats of southern New Mexico, taking the old ranch roads north. To where, he asked himself? Alamogordo, Artesia? Better than going back to the main highway. His thoughts were coming hard and fast but they weren't helping him. They weren't solving his problem.

"Times must have been different back then." The waitress was still standing there looking at him.

"What?"

"I said that I bet things were different back then, when you lived here." There was that smile again.

"Oh yeah, things were very different then." He counted out money for the bill, leaving her a good tip.

He was trying to remember where it was that he had to turn to get on the old ranch road that led to the Alamogordo highway. He thought about Old Ralph and an image formed of the old man taking nineteen thousand dollars and leaving the one thousand in the old tin box. He supposed he should be grateful to the old man for leaving him enough for gas and a decent getaway, but he couldn't find it in him.

47

LAST GAME
AT KEZAR

The winter fog, wet and clean, came in through the Golden Gate and covered the dark streets of North Beach. The foghorn boomed out its warning in a regular cadence, its deep base note cutting through the cold mist. Johnny sat at the wheel of his uncle's Buick a few doors down from the Italian Athletic Club. It irritated him that he was wasting his Saturday night, but he had no choice in the matter. Uncle Dom had instructed him to find Gino and bring him to the warehouse on the Wharf. He had been enjoying himself, sitting at the bar of his favorite café, talking with the bartender who took book from a few trusted souls in the neighborhood. Johnny had been trying, with no luck, to get better odds on the game tomorrow but was finally satisfied that he had gotten three points. Vegas had the Niners plus four, but no bookie in the City would give these odds since nearly all of the bettors were putting their money on the 49ers. The bartender had told Johnny that even the big bookies had to lay off to the banks down south in order to balance their books. He and the bartender had been talking about the Niners' chances when the bar phone rang. The bartender had answered and then handed the phone to Johnny.

"Find Gino and bring him to that place on the Wharf. You know which one!" Uncle Dom had hung up without waiting for a reply. That's the way it was with Uncle Dom. He gave the orders and Johnny carried them out. He could not remember ever having a real conversation with his uncle. So now, here he was across from Washington Square looking for Gino. He had nothing against Gino; in fact, they had been close in their younger years when they had shared a passion for soccer and had played together on the same teams from the youth leagues all the way up to the city league. Gino was a speedy forward who could deliver a powerful shot on goal with either foot. Johnny played center back and held the league record for penalties, even being suspended for an entire season because of his physical style of play. The other teams might score against Johnny's back line but they always paid the price. Gino was the top scorer in the league year after year, and always wore a smirk on his handsome face after he scored a goal. He had that cocky attitude that irritated a lot of the older people in the neighborhood, but they overlooked it because he brought them a bit of fame, something they could brag about in the North Beach bars and cafés.

After they hung up their cleats they drifted apart, only seeing one another at weddings or during big North Beach celebrations like Columbus Day. Gino went to City College and then to UC on the other side of the Bay. He became an accountant and went to work for Uncle Dom. Johnny also went to work for his uncle. After dropping out of high school and being turned down by the military because of a bum knee, he began unloading crabs and fish from his uncle's boats on the Wharf. After Johnny spent a year proving to his uncle that he could work hard and keep his mouth shut, Uncle Dom and his associates found another use for Johnny's strength and aggressive nature. This had changed his life. He was soon making enough money to move out of the basement apartment he shared with a cousin over on Greenwich Street. He now had his own place, could afford nice clothes, and his social life had improved since he no longer stank of fish. And all he had to do to keep this lifestyle was follow his uncle's orders and not get involved with the punks who thought that they knew better. Like Gino.

Johnny watched an old priest come out of the cathedral across the square and lock the doors. The spires of the cathedral were hidden by the fog. The mist hung around the old streetlamps and the light formed concentric circles of various shades of white and pink around each pointed globe. The old lamps stood like tall, thin ghosts in a line down Stockton Street where, in the distance, the circles were eaten up by the fog. When Johnny was a boy and the nuns marched his class up Filbert Street, the Sisters said the colored circles reminded them of the "crown of the Virgin Mary." Johnny remembered thinking that only a nun would link the fog to religion. As for him, when the fog was in on North Beach it made the tissues in his sinuses swell and it was hard for him to breathe.

He didn't know what Gino might have done to be called to the Wharf. He only knew that he had heard a rumor earlier in the day that his uncle had sent for the brothers from South City, and whenever the brothers were sent for, there was a serious problem. When he had heard this rumor, he had no idea that Gino was involved, but Johnny, like everyone who knew Uncle Dom, could not help but feel a sense of relief that the brothers were not there for him, and at the same time he felt a measure of pity for whoever the brothers would be talking to.

He didn't know why Uncle Dom wanted Gino at the Wharf. Was he a snitch? Did they catch him wetting his beak in the company funds? Johnny didn't know. In fact, it didn't matter. Whatever complication Gino had gotten himself into was not Johnny's concern. He was only here to make sure Gino was delivered to a meeting on the Wharf.

In a little while he saw Gino come out of a club with a girl. She was a pretty blond, tall and slim with short hair. Probably a Paddy broad from the Mission, he thought. That would be Gino's style. Johnny got out of the car and stood next to it, his feet on the sidewalk. He did not want the girl to get a good look at him. He fought a sneeze from his tortured sinuses and called Gino by name. Gino stopped and looked down the street in his direction. He told the girl to wait and then walked down the street to Johnny.

"Uncle Dom sent me," Johnny told him. It was all that was necessary. Anyone in his uncle's world knew what that meant.

"Give me a minute!" Gino went back to the girl, grabbed her by the arm and steered her to the front door of the club. He spoke a few words that Johnny could not hear, kissed her on the cheek, and after she went back inside the club, he turned and walked down the street to the Buick. They were silent as they got into the car and Johnny drove north on Stockton past the cathedral. The fog limited visibility to a few blocks and the world of North Beach closed in on both of them.

"Do you know what it's about, Johnny?" Gino tried to act unconcerned but Johnny heard the stress in his voice.

"No. Nobody tells me anything." He kept his eyes on the road.

"We goin' to the Wharf?"

He knows, thought Johnny. He damn sure knows. He did not answer Gino's question.

"I heard the brothers were in the City. Is that true?" Gino's voice took on a higher note.

Dammit, Johnny thought, now I'm starting to feel sorry for him. "Yeah, Gino. I heard that he sent for them." He didn't feel guilty telling Gino that. After all, they couldn't prove he talked about something that was already a rumor in the bars of North Beach. Gino was quiet for a few blocks.

"You goin' to the game tomorrow?" Gino's voice was almost back to normal.

"Nah, couldn't get tickets. Nobody can get tickets."

"I think the Niners will take 'em. Brodie is looking good, like his shoulder's not bothering him anymore."

They were quiet for a while longer and when Johnny turned left on to Bay Street, Gino asked him: "Would you tell me if you knew I was in trouble?"

"Dammit, Gino. You know how it is!"

Gino reached inside his jacket and Johnny turned to him quickly. He took his right hand off the wheel, and grabbed Gino's wrist, his right foot stabbed the brake pedal.

"Relax Gian Luca! I just wanted to give you this." He handed Johnny an envelope.

"What the hell is this?" Johnny felt the sweat break out in his armpits. If it had anything to do with the situation Gino was involved in, Johnny did not want any part of it.

"Two tickets to the game tomorrow. I was going to take the blonde you saw me with. Anyway, take whoever you want. It'll be the Niners' last game out at Kezar, you know." Gino sat back.

"Gino, I really don't know what the hell is going on. Uncle Dom just told me to find you and bring you to the Wharf." Johnny slipped the envelope into his jacket.

Gino remained silent, looking straight ahead. He looked tired.

"Gino! Do yourself a favor, show them some respect! Don't be your usual cocky self. You know how these guys are. Just show respect and don't try to lie to them. Whatever this is about, they'll know more than you."

"Thanks, Gian Luca. I'll do that."

"Good. I'll hold the tickets and give them back to you in the morning."

He glanced over at Gino, who was definitely not his usual overconfident self. He was not the boy who always thought he could talk his way into and out of anything.

He turned onto Beach Street and drove to a warehouse a few blocks from the chocolate factory. There was a smaller door cut into the large warehouse door and Johnny recognized one of the brothers standing in front.

"Ciao, Gino." Johnny nodded toward the warehouse.

Gino looked at him and said nothing. There was a serious look in his eye as if he were making up his mind about something. He sat very still for a moment and then got out of the car. Silently, Johnny wished Gino luck and hoped that his way with words would make this go away but he knew that when the brothers from South City were sent for, the time for talking was over. They would get whatever information they needed from Gino and pull the trigger at the same time the foghorn boomed. They would take Gino out on one of the boats from the fishing fleet. They would take him out past the Farallones before dawn and Gino's name would never be mentioned again.

Johnny turned onto Hyde Street and crossed the cable car turnaround at the foot of the hill. He felt the rear of the car slide as he accelerated across the wet steel plating of the turnaround and then steady out as he slowed for the stop sign. He looked south up the hill. The cable car tracks were wet and reflected a hard, cold, blue-black color as they ran up the hill out of sight into the mist. He wondered if it was too late to get a plate of clams at D'Nunzios. He turned left onto Bay, crossed the tracks again and heard the fog horn's deep bass note as he headed back to North Beach.

FOLLOWING THE
HARVEST

The summer of 1964 was coming to a close in South Texas and it was raining. The harvesting of feed crops was over and the combining crew would follow the harvest north where the fields matured later in the year. Josh would not be going with them. He sat at a table in the equipment barn eating a bologna sandwich and cold potatoes from last night's supper. It would be the last meal provided by the company. He would begin his trip home today and as he finished his meal his thoughts were filled with football practice and the beginning of his junior year in high school. On the table next to his paper plate sat a small canvas grip that held his work clothes and three hundred and ninety-four dollars, his pay for the last eight weeks, minus the room and board charges that he owed the company. He finished his meal and walked over to the front of the barn where the foreman's pickup was parked. The foreman had promised him a ride to the bus station in town, and while Josh waited for him he transferred his cash from the grip to his billfold. As he felt the heavy bulge in his back pocket, he remembered what the foreman had told him about not letting anybody know how much money he was carrying. He watched the rain fall on the combines and other farm equipment and puddle in the low spots of the dirt lot. The rain did not cool the air, it only made it heavier. Nor did it relieve the itching caused by the eight weeks of plant chaff that felt as if it was buried deep under his skin. He stood there scratching his neck, feeling the warm dampness rise from the ground up his body, making his clothes sag heavily against his itching skin. He hated South Texas.

The bus depot was a small room in the same building as the Sears and Roebuck showroom. There were no busses in sight. Just a cardboard sign with the Trailways logo painted on it.

Josh walked into the bus station. The ticket agent sat at a metal desk behind the small counter and did not get up as Josh walked up to him.

"The last bus left two hours ago and there won't be another 'til ten tomorrow morning. If you can make your way to Uvalde, we have a bigger station there and you can catch a bus to almost anywhere you want to go."

Josh walked outside and stood under the overhang in front of the station and watched the rain come down. A police car drove by slowly and the officer gave Josh a good long look. Well, he thought, I ain't getting anything done just standing here watching it rain. He decided that since there was plenty of daylight left, he would get out on the highway and hitch a ride to Uvalde.

The rain let up to a light drizzle, and as he walked several blocks down the main street of town the police car he had seen earlier pulled up behind him. He turned around to face the officer as he got out of his car.

"Where you going?" The officer was a tall young man and Josh didn't think he was too friendly.

"I'm trying to get to Uvalde."

"Why?"

"To catch a bus."

"A bus to where?"

"El Paso."

"What did you lose in El Paso?"

"I didn't lose anything there but it's close to home. I tried to catch a bus here but the last one just left."

"I think you better come with me."

"Why? I didn't do anything wrong."

"I'll decide that. Now get in the back of my vehicle."

Josh watched the officer approach him. Vehicle? Who talked like that? Josh walked to the back of the officer's car.

Josh sat in the back seat and watched the store fronts pass by in the rain. The police car smelled of cigarette smoke and sweat. They drove past the front of the police station, a two-story, tan brick building and turned into an alley halfway down the block. The officer parked the car in a large lot with a chain-link fence on all four sides. Another policeman came out of the back door of the police building. He stopped and watched Josh get out of the car.

"What you got there Anderson?"

"A vagrant." Anderson replied. He held onto Josh's small grip. "In there!" He pointed to the door the other officer had just exited.

"You sure he's just a vagrant, Anderson? Looks like he just got out of prison. Probably a dangerous desperado or maybe a homicidal maniac! And you don't even have him cuffed? You old enough to shave son?" The other officer laughed out loud and got into his police car.

Josh took some pleasure in seeing Anderson blush.

"What we got Anderson?" A uniformed sergeant looked up from his desk as they came into the office. There was a wooden sign on the desk with the name: "Sgt. Lorenzo de la Garza." There was a secretary at another desk near the front door.

"I think we got a vagrant, Sarge."

"But I ain't no—"

"Hush up, son," the sergeant told Josh. "I'll get to you in a minute. Where did you find him Anderson?"

"On Main near the bus station." As they were talking, an older man came in through the front door. He was dressed in a suit and was smoking a pipe.

"Good evening, Sergeant. Officer Anderson." He greeted the two officers but his eyes studied Josh.

"Evening, Judge." Both officers nodded to the man.

"This man under arrest, Sergeant?"

"Yessir." Anderson spoke before the sergeant could reply.

"On what charge?"

"Vagrancy, Your Honor." Anderson stood at attention.

"I see. Well, I'll be in the courtroom when you need me."
The man walked down a hallway into another office and closed
the door behind him.

"Put him in the holding cell, Anderson." The sergeant had a
look of disgust on his face.

"But I haven't told you my side yet." Josh spoke over his
shoulder as Anderson led him to the holding cell.

"You'll get your chance in a minute!" The sergeant said.

After Josh was put in the cell, the sergeant called officer
Anderson to his desk.

"Where was he going?"

"Claimed he was going to hitch a ride to Uvalde, Sarge."

"And why didn't you let him?"

"What? I mean . . . well I—"

"Anderson! Did it ever occur to you that once he was outside
the city limits and on his way to Uvalde, he would not be our
problem? Now we're going to have to print him, book him,
feed him, and house him. My jail budget is shot to hell and you
load me up with another nonpaying ward of the city."

"But Sarge, I—"

"Get out of here Anderson! Get back on patrol and if you see
any more vagrants, escort them all the damn way out of my town."

"Yes, Sarge." Anderson gave Josh a hard look as he walked
past the cell on his way back to patrol.

The sergeant walked over to Josh's cell opened the door and
stepped in. "Josh, I'm Sergeant de la Garza. I'll need to see your
driver's license."

Josh reached into his back pocket and removed his billfold.
As he was taking out his license the sergeant noticed the money.

"How much money you got there, Josh?"

"Almost four hundred dollars." He held the billfold out to Sergeant de la Garza.

"No, Josh. I won't touch it but I need you to pull out that cash, count it, and lay it on the bunk there so I can get a good look."

Josh did as he was told and after the sergeant was satisfied, he told Josh to put it back into his billfold and put the billfold back in his pocket. Then the sergeant began asking Josh a lot of questions.

Later, after he had finished his questions and locked Josh in the cell, the sergeant looked over his desk at the teenager. Country boy, he thought, not a city boy. His pride will get him in trouble someday but there was no guile in him. He was honest to the point of being naïve. He had answered the sergeant's questioning without holding anything back. The sergeant tested him in all the ways he had learned over the years but the boy was steadfast in his answers. He only rose to the bait one time when the sergeant probed around points of his honesty and his pride. He did not book Josh into the system since he knew the judge would have to release him.

And now it was time to take him before the newly elected justice of the peace who had let everyone know that he preferred to be called "Your Honor." Only dimwits like Anderson eagerly called him that. To the sergeant he would always be judge with a small "j." He would reserve "Your Honor" for the real judges in criminal court.

"The sergeant told me he has discovered close to four hundred dollars in your billfold. Where did you get that kind of money?" The judge looked sternly at Josh.

"I worked for Carter Custom Combines this summer and that money is eight weeks wages minus room and board, sir." Josh turned and looked at the sergeant. "I told Sergeant de la Garza where I was working and when I got paid off and came into town."

"Sergeant?"

"I called out there and spoke with the foreman who verified this boy's identity and also his pay."

"So it appears that you are not a vagrant." The judge studied some papers on his desk, shuffling them around for a full minute before looking up at Josh. "There will be no charges filed against you. You are free to go."

"Thank you, sir."

"And Sergeant, before releasing this boy please ensure that he pays court costs of thirty-seven dollars and fifty cents. Also, please ensure that he is given an official receipt."

While Josh counted out the court fees to the sergeant, the judge walked through the police office and at the front door turned and announced: "Goodnight, Mrs. Wilson. Sergeant."

"Good night, Judge." They both responded. After the judge closed the door, Mrs. Wilson gave the sergeant a knowing look and continued typing up the receipt for Josh.

"What'll you do now, Josh?" The sergeant handed back all of Josh's belongings.

"Hitch a ride to Uvalde and catch a bus."

"It's getting late and the highway is no place to be on foot at this time of day. If you don't have a place to stay the night, you could stay in one of our regular cells in the back. Can't feed you or give you clean sheets but there are a couple of clean blankets back there. You can go out and get something to eat and come back."

"Sounds good to me. Thanks, Sergeant."

When Josh left, Mrs. Wilson brought the receipt over to the sergeant.

"Goodness Larry, you're getting soft in your old age."

"The old man took nearly four day's wages off that boy with no good reason. So I'm just trying to even things out a little."

"Well, Larry, you should know by now that nothing good comes of doing good deeds."

Sergeant de la Garza shook his head as Mrs. Wilson walked back to her desk. There was no doubt that she was long overdue for retirement. He read the receipt very carefully.

———————

It was still drizzling when Josh left the police station in the morning. As he made his way down Main Street toward the bus station it began to rain harder. He passed an alley and spotted an old building that looked like an abandoned garage at the far end. A large wooden door hung open at the front of it. He hurried over and slipped in next to the broken door. He was out of the rain but it felt damp inside the building, just like all of South Texas, he thought. It was a large building and as his eyes adjusted to the darkness, he smelled wood smoke. At the far end of the building, he could make out a figure of someone with a blanket over his or her shoulders.

"Hello?" he hollered.

"Hello yourself. Come on over!" It was a girl's voice.

He slowly edged around to the far side, hugging the wall where there was less trash and debris. As he got close to the fire, he saw a girl with long blond hair and a large blanket wrapped around her. She was holding the blanket closed at her throat. The rest of the blanket hung open and he could see she was completely naked underneath the blanket. She caught his look and pointed to the wall on the other side of the fire. A pair of jeans, a shirt, and pieces of female underwear hung on several large spikes that had been driven into the wall.

"You can hang yours up there if you want."

"Thanks, but I'm not that wet." He felt his face flush in the dim light.

"I got some corned beef warming on the fire. Hungry?"

"Thanks, but I just ate." He saw an army mess kit balanced on a rock at the edge of the fire.

"My name is Jacqueline, but you can call me Jackie." She smiled at Josh.

"My name is Josh." He almost stuttered as the blanket billowed open every time Jackie moved. It did not seem to bother her that she was almost completely uncovered. Then to his pleasant surprise, she took off the blanket, folded it neatly, placed it on a dusty, upended box, and walked, naked, over to the wall to retrieve her clothes. Josh tried to look away but found that he could not. She was beautiful with a young, firm body that stood out white against the damp gloom of the old garage. She took each article of clothing from the wall, examined it for dryness and put it on.

"You look like a moron standing there with your mouth open. Have you never seen a naked woman?"

"Well, no, I haven't."

"Don't make a big deal of it. Cute as you are, you'll probably see your share. Where you headed?" she pointed to Josh's
grip.

"I was walking to the bus station."

"And where was this bus to take you?"

"El Paso."

"Only bus from here goes to Uvalde or Eagle Pass. Why you
going to El Paso?"

"It's close to home."

"I can take you to Uvalde and you can catch a bus to El
Paso from there. I got a pickup out back, it's just little low on
gas. Got any money? I mean, you don't expect to ride free, do
you?"

"No, I have some money."

"How much?" She smiled at him. There was something about
the smile. He couldn't place it but he remembered the warning
the foreman had given him that morning.

"Just about enough for gas." He had to make a choice. Take
a chance catching a bus in this small town again or ride straight
through to Uvalde with the most beautiful girl he had ever seen.
Not much of a choice but there was still something about her
that made him uneasy.

"Well, let's go then." Jackie kicked the mess kit and meat
into the fire and began to kick dirt over the small flames.

A new GMC pickup truck sat under a tree behind the old
garage. The spare tire still had a sticker plastered over the tread.
As he climbed in on the passenger side, he noticed a dark stain
on the driver's side of the seat. Jackie caught his look.

"Deer blood. My uncle is real careless. This is his truck and sometimes, I swear, he doesn't take care of things the way he should."

"Deer season's not 'til December." He looked at her.

"Uncle Joe spotlights them whenever he needs meat. If you are afraid of a little deer blood, you don't have to come along."

"No, I'm OK. You're right, your uncle should take better care of his things."

Jackie was quiet as she drove. She had a heavy foot and after they passed the city limits of the small town, she sped down the highway to Uvalde. She began to talk again.

"Do you have a steady girlfriend, Josh?"

"No. Not really."

"Not really, huh?" she laughed. "I doubt that but let me tell you a story. The truth about why I have my uncle's pickup, OK?"

"OK."

"I'm running away, Josh. Running away from a bad situation. See, it's like this. I was supposed to get married to this guy. My family was all for it. He had lots of money, a big ranch and all that. But I didn't love him. Hell, I didn't even like him. So how could I marry somebody like that? I mean, could you?"

"No, I don't believe I could."

"See! I knew you'd understand. Me? I would like to just keep on going. Out of Texas, maybe all the way to California. I've got money, don't need anybody to pay my way. And I wouldn't have anybody telling me what to do and who I should marry!"

"Sounds good. Kinda like a dream."

"I could get a job, stay someplace until I get tired of it, then move on to someplace else. What about you? You just gonna stay in boring old El Paso and do boring things the rest of your life?"

"Well no, but I . . . ." Her tone rankled him but this small bit of annoyance was quickly pushed aside by a vision of him lying next to Jackie on a beach in California, watching the waves roll in. He had never even been close to a beach but the thought of Jackie in a bikini made everything seem possible.

"I know you're a nice guy, I could tell when I saw you walk into that old garage. Then I saw you looking at me when I was naked and you didn't try anything. I knew then you were a real gentleman who wouldn't take advantage. Tell you the truth Josh, I kinda fell for you." She turned and smiled at him.

Josh's mind was spinning. He had never had so many different ideas put in his head at the same time. He tried to slow his thinking by watching the road. After a while they entered the outskirts of Uvalde and by then Josh had decided that he would ride with her to El Paso. California? He was tempted but had not made up his mind.

"Oh damn!" Jackie shouted.

Josh looked at her. "What is it?"

"The gauge is sitting on empty. I forget about the gas!"

"Pull into the next gas station and we'll fill it up." Josh spotted a Fina station several blocks down the street. "There's one up ahead and there's a café too. While they're filling it up, I'll get us some food to take with us." He looked at Jackie with her long hair down over her shoulders and her eyes, a light blue that made him feel weak inside. He could hear the Pacific Ocean crashing on the beach as she stopped in front of the pump island at the gas station. She looked into his eyes and gave him her big beautiful smile.

"Does this mean that I'm not dropping you at the bus station?"

"Look, I'm not sure about going to California, but I will ride with you to El Paso." He had almost reached the point of no return because he didn't really care about all the other things in his life. Right now, the only thing he wanted was to be with her. He needed time to think, to plan. His mind would have to stop swirling around before he could think clearly, that was for sure. But in the meantime, he told himself, I will be with her. God, when he looked into her eyes, he just went all soft, like he was melting.

"Don't you worry Josh, I know some back roads out of this town that will get us to the main highway in a hurry, and before you know it you and me will be on our way!"

"What can I do for you folks?" The attendant was standing at the driver's door, his eyes on Jackie, ignoring Josh.

"Fill it up please." Jackie smiled at him and the attendant dropped the red rag he held in his left hand then bumped his head on the pickup door when he bent to retrieve it.

"Yes, ma'am!"

"I'll go get us a couple of burgers and pay for the gas when I get back." Josh opened the passenger door.

"Don't you think you ought to leave me the money to pay for the gas?" Jackie asked him.

"I'll pay when I get back. That OK with you?" he asked the attendant.

"You bet!" He was trying to get a better look at Jackie from where he stood at the truck's gas tank.

Jackie was quiet as she sat with her hands on the steering wheel. Josh jogged over to the café, his mind already out on the highway riding west into the sunset, sitting next to Jackie. He could smell the beef and onions frying on the grill as he got close to the café. The cooking smells made him hungry and as his appetite increased, his concerns for the future diminished. The things that caused the little warning signals to rise in his head faded away and his thoughts were now filled with the picture of him and Jackie floating down the highway heading to a place where dreams live.

There were a few people at the counter inside the café but all the tables and booths were empty. As he sat down on a stool at the counter, the two other customers got up. He looked up at the waiter and was about to give him his order when he noticed the waiter's eyes widen and then he felt an iron grip on each of his arms.

"Police officers! Don't struggle and keep your mouth shut!" The voice was quiet but firm. His arms were pulled behind him and he felt metal being placed on his wrists and then he heard a clicking sound as the handcuffs were tightened.

"Just sit there, son, and listen to me. Where does your girl-friend keep the gun?"

"Gun? What gun? My girlfriend?" Josh's head swam and then a voice came from near the front door.

"It's OK, Sarge, they got her!"

The two officers who had handcuffed him lifted him from the stool and led him to the front door. Another officer opened the door and he was led outside. He could hear Jackie screaming and shouting across the way at the gas station. She was handcuffed and two police officers were pulling her toward their cruiser. As they held her, and as she cursed them and continued to struggle, another officer grabbed her thrashing legs and cinched a heavy leather belt over her ankles. They put her in the back seat and closed the door.

Josh recognized Sergeant de la Garza among the police officers near Jackie's pickup truck. He spotted Josh and walked over to him and the other officers.

"Josh? What the hell you doin' with her?"

"You know this kid, Larry?"

"Yeah, I know him. It's a long story." He looked at Josh and shook his head. "I'll follow you downtown and we'll interview him there. I don't know what's going on but he's not her type. I think he's all right but just the same keep the cuffs on him 'til we get downtown."

At the police station Sergeant de la Garza explained to Josh that he and the other officers from several departments were working together on this case. Then he asked Josh to tell him everything that happened from the moment he left the police station until he and Jackie pulled into the gas station. As Josh told his story, they took the cuffs off and brought him a cup of coffee and a candy bar. They then took him to a cell and closed and locked the door.

"It'll just be a little while, Josh. They'll bring you some food in a bit and then I'll come back and process your release. I gotta ask you this, Josh: did you have intimate relations with this girl?"

"Intimate? You mean—? No, no, I didn't. Why?"

"Did you give her any of your money? Do you still have your money?"

"I still have all of it. I didn't give her any of it."

"Good. I'll be back in a while. Relax, Josh, you're not in any trouble, we just have to tie up a few loose ends. One other thing. A nurse will be here in a minute to draw your blood."

Josh tried to relax but his mind was a swirl of confusion. Then the nurse came with a big needle and a couple of small vials. It was the first time he had ever had blood taken but he was relieved that it was not as bad as he thought it would be when he first saw the needle. There were still a hundred questions. Why did they arrest Jackie? Who was she and what had she done? As his mind ran in circles and he kept asking himself the same questions, it slowly dawned on him that his dreams of riding away with Jackie, of being with her, being free with her, all of those images had fled his mind so quickly he began to wonder if he ever had them at all.

After about five hours, Sergeant de la Garza and another man in plain clothes came and got Josh out of the cell and took him to an office that had a wooden desk and chairs, a sofa, and paintings on the wall.

"Josh, this is Lieutenant Wells and he is in charge of the investigation. He'll explain what this all about."

"Josh, the girl you know as Jackie is actually one Christine Dobbs. She also goes by a few other names but that doesn't matter. Right now, what does matter is that Miss Dobbs shot and killed a man on the outskirts of Laredo yesterday. She is a well-known, high-end prostitute and he was in the process of picking her up when it happened. It appears that she was in his pickup when she shot him at close range, removed him from the pickup truck and took off with his truck, his billfold, and his money. We found the gun stuck down in the seat on the driver's side of the truck and his billfold in her bag. It appears to be the same gun used in two other murders in the area. Both of these deceased victims were also males, probably engaged in similar arrangements with Miss Dobbs. We are in the process of putting all of that together as we speak. Miss Dobbs had been working out of a fancy house in Laredo. She was very expensive and dealt only with those who could afford her. Things began to go south for her several months ago when she contracted a real bad strain of syphilis and passed it along to several clients of this fancy house. You have heard of this disease?"

"Yes, sir."

"Well then, you know how serious it is. That is why you had your blood drawn. The lab is working overtime to get the results so you can get out of here and be on your way. Sorry, Josh, we can't release you until the results are back. The state health authorities have come down hard on this case and are trying to isolate anyone who may have had contact with Miss Dobbs. Anyway, one of the other victims was found outside Carrizo Springs and one outside of Eagle Pass. They were found on back roads way out in the country. Did Miss Dobbs mention those two towns or any of her travels?"

"No, sir. She never told me anything about herself, except that she was going to be married and that the pickup truck belonged to her uncle. There was a big stain on the front seat that she said was blood from a deer that her uncle spotlighted."

"The stain is human blood. We know that much and are certain it belongs to the victim. The lab boys are narrowing that down now. Look, Josh, Sergeant de la Garza tells me that you're a good kid so I don't want to alarm you, but there is no doubt in my mind that she planned to take you to some remote spot on a back road, shoot you, and take your money." He looked at Josh a long moment. "Well, that's about it. Got any questions for me?"

"No, sir." Josh felt all the strength go out of him and he leaned back in the chair.

"Good. As soon as your blood test results are back you are free to go." The Lieutenant picked up a file of papers and left the room.

Several hours later Sergeant de la Garza came to the cell where Josh had been placed while awaiting the blood test results.

"Well, Josh, everything checks out fine just as I figured. So let's get you over to the bus station. The El Paso bus leaves in two hours so that'll give us time to get you checked out of here."

It was not far to the bus station and they arrived with an hour to spare and then sat in the police car in front of the station. Sergeant de la Garza pointed to a café across the street from the bus station.

"See that café over there?"

"Yes, sir."

"Whatever you do, don't eat there. Worst food in town." Josh didn't answer. He was looking straight ahead out the front windshield. "Josh, I noticed that you never asked the lieutenant about what would happen to Jackie."

"I guess I don't really care. She's like a bad dream now and I just want to be as far away from her and this place as possible."

"People like her are a bad dream, but the good news is that here we are, you are still alive and getting on a bus that will put some distance between you and a nightmare. You hit a lucky streak, because if just a few things had gone differently—if you had slept with her or if we had missed y'all at the gas station and she had taken the back roads out of town—well, about now we would have been trying to identify your remains and connect you with the other victims. So, all in all, fortune has smiled on you. I sure hope you'll keep that in mind."

"Yes, sir, I will." The silence between them became awkward. "You sure the El Paso bus leaves at seven?"

"Sure as I'm sitting here. I put my oldest son on it last Tuesday."

"He was going to El Paso?"

"Reporting to Fort Bliss, being shipped out." The sergeant suddenly looked older to Josh. His face was tight. "You take care of yourself, Josh." They shook hands and Josh got out of the car. He watched Sergeant de la Garza drive off and then went inside the bus station.

Josh had twenty minutes to spare after he bought his ticket so he strolled over to the double doors that led to the lot where the buses were parked. He thought of the money in his billfold and how it would set him up for a while. He would add to it by fixing flats and pumping gas at the El Paso Red Flame after school. His thoughts were not as heavy now as he thought of home and all the things that were familiar to him and of getting as far away from South Texas as possible. He definitely felt very lucky about Jackie or whatever her name was. He sat alone on one of the wooden benches and his thoughts returned to a time long ago when he sat with his mother in another bus station in Texas and of all the things that had happened since then.

"Are these places taken?" A pleasant female voice brought him back from his memories. An older woman standing next to blond teenage girl smiled and pointed to the place on the bench next to Josh.

"No, ma'am." He stood as they carried their suitcases past him and sat down. The pretty young blond sat next to Josh.

"Thank you, young man. Are you going to El Paso?" the older woman asked.

"Yes, ma'am." He looked at her and then at the young girl. She had blue eyes and a pretty smile. She reminded him of Jackie and his stomach tightened. She reached into her purse and brought out a pack of gum. She carefully unwrapped it and pulled a stick part way out of the pack and offered it to Josh.

"No, thank you," he stammered. He felt a dampness form in his armpits and could feel his heart beat in his dry throat. He reached down and picked up his grip. "I forgot. I have to make a call." He stumbled a bit as he stood. "I'll see y'all on the bus." He turned and walked away as the older lady frowned.

As he walked around the corner and out of their sight, he fought to control his panic, telling himself that he could not continue to react like this every time he saw a girl that reminded him of Jackie. When it was time to board the bus, he had calmed down. He stood near the front of the line of passengers and looked back to see the woman and the young girl near the end of the line. They looked like the type that preferred to sit in the back of the bus, away from the driver and the opening and closing of the door. In a few minutes, they began to board and Josh grabbed the seat right behind the driver. He pretended to be looking at something outside the bus, avoiding eye contact with the boarding passengers. He knew it was going to be a long ride to El Paso.

CHAPO

Chapo sat his horse in a clearing on a small hill and watched Jones ride away on the far side of the broken ground at the foot of the mountains. Jones was on his way to a white man's city where he would get on a train and ride to another city in search of the bad man. This time Chapo would not go with him. The whites called Chapo's home Arizona Territory, and the men, like Jones, who wore the badge, Arizona Rangers. This man Jones was one of two whites Chapo respected. The other was General Crook. He had hunted men with both of them.

He and Jones had said goodbye when the sun was halfway down and clouds were building over the mountains. They heard the faint rumble of thunder as Jones tried to convince Chapo to come with him.

"It will be a good hunt for a very bad man," the Ranger said. Chapo had seen the truth in the Ranger's eyes and he felt the old thrill of the hunt and the adventure of going with him to find the bad man. But as he tried to form the words, he knew that he would not.

"I cannot hunt in your cities. I hunt here. I stay here. This is how I must do." It pained him to decline, for he had good memories of his last hunt with this Ranger, but his vision was clear that he would be lost in the white man's cities.

He watched until Jones was a small figure on the horizon and then he felt the stab of pain return. It began, as always, in his bowels, and moved up his right side and would stay awhile before subsiding. It had been with him for months and the intensity of the pain had increased over that time. But this did not worry him for he had a plan to cure it.

As a young boy he had been taught the ways of a hunter, for it was the way of his people, and when he was old enough he began his tests as a warrior with the other young boys. One winter they had traveled to a stream that ran through the trees high in the mountains. The old ones, his father among them, had the boys build a fire on a high bank next to the stream. He remembered the snow swirling quietly in the breeze and then he and the other boys were made to strip and step into the middle of the stream where the water was almost to their shoulders. He had never felt such cold. It numbed him and he remembered being afraid that he would stumble because he could not feel his feet. He and the other boys stood, waiting for the old ones to speak, but they were talking among themselves by the fire, ignoring the boys in the stream. Finally, after a long time one of the old men waved at the boys to come out. Some of the boys rushed out of the stream and ran, shivering, to the fire. Chapo waited. He wanted to be the last one out. And when all the other boys were out and by the fire he climbed the high bank, holding his jaws tight to keep his teeth from chattering, and walked slowly over to the fire. He remembered standing there with the snowflakes coming down thick and white, disappearing as they hissed into the fire. He looked away from the fire, faking a disinterest in its warmth and his gaze went to the men standing by his father, and he thought he saw approval in their eyes.

Now he would return to that stream and let the waters cool this burning pain and take it out of him and make him young again.

Among his people, there were things that were forbidden. Taboos. Without letting the old ones know, he had always chosen which of these taboos he would observe. One of several he followed was that he never ate fish or anything that lived in water. But the one that he ignored was one of the most powerful of all the taboos. His people believed the color red attracted lightning and they taught their young to avoid wearing that color when storms came. He would secretly go off by himself during thunderstorms wearing a red headband, tempting the gods. He would stand in a clearing, look up at the clouds, and dare them to strike him down, but they never did. At first, he thought that the spirits had favored him, but as he aged, he finally accepted that maybe there was nothing to the taboo after all.

After Jones had faded over the horizon, he turned his horse and faced the mountains where the clouds were darkening. He pulled a red headband out of a chamois sack, folded it carefully, and put it to his forehead, tying it tight behind his head. He thought back to the time General Crook made all the scouts wear the red headband so that the white soldiers would not mistake them for renegades they hunted, and how during all the time he had worn it he had never been hurt. Not even a scratch.

And now he saw lightning flash in the distance and knew it would be raining in the high country and the old stream would be running full. He chuckled to himself, feeling the carelessness of his youth, and as he dug his heels into his horse's flank and began his climb, he was laughing out loud.

IMPERFECTIONS

It had not been Domingo's intention to beat Luisa as badly as he did. He only meant it as a lesson to her and the other girls at the Club Azul. But Luisa had remained defiant during his exertions and had looked at him with disdain, her dark eyes not flinching even after he was sure that he had broken one of her ribs. It was as if she witnessed the beating from afar, passive in her contempt of him. Her lack of fear only increased his own, the one that he kept locked deep inside and away from the others in his world. So he lost his control and punished her far more than he had planned. His rage finally subsided when he felt the strength go out of his arms and he realized he would only look weak to the other girls if he continued with less vigor. Domingo was respected in this business and he could not let this little puta challenge his authority in front of the others. Lately she had become very particular about which customers she would take to the back room, and he could not tolerate that. Later, he realized that he had caused enough damage to her face that she probably would not be able to work for a long time, but the owner had always given him total discretion in managing the workforce. Besides, with her sullen attitude and short, blunt build she was not what you would call a real money maker. So it was of no matter to him if she went back to the mountains and took her insolence with her. He had a business to run.

The first week of Luisa's recovery comprised days with no structure. She would regain consciousness and be completely owned by the pain. She was not aware of time or whether it was dark or light, she only felt the pain. When she finally regained a small piece of reasoning, her foremost thought was of wanting to die so she could escape the pain. The headaches stayed with her as the open wounds scabbed over and the color of the bruises changed from dark blue to light yellow.

Her good friend, Elvita, had put her up at her place, a two-room apartment out in the colonias. There was running water but no electricity. Luisa had no place of her own and had lived in a room above the Club Azul with two other girls who did not have enough money for their own apartment. Elvita had gone to the club and retrieved Luisa's small suitcase that held everything she owned. Elvita's cousin, a nurse at the Hospital Seguridad Social in the central district, brought pills that dulled the pain and had stitched up some of the worst of her wounds. The cousin was concerned about the eventual scarring that would occur, especially on Luisa's face.

But Luisa did not care about that, she only wanted the pain to go away and to get well enough to leave Ciudad Juarez.

Elvita worked at the Café Siempre on a street just off Avenida Juarez, and after her shift she would take the streetcar to the end of the line and then a bus out to the colonias. She brought food for Luisa. At first it was only the broth from caldo de res, but after a week Luisa was able to eat the meat and vegetables in the soup. After three weeks, she was able to stand and take a few steps around the tiny room, but it wasn't until the fifth week that she was able to go outside and sit in the courtyard of the building and let the sun wash over her body. It was then that she knew she would be all right. Elvita talked with her long into the night until pain pills made Luisa sleepy and then Elvita would sleep on a mat on the floor and listen to Luisa's moans and her mumblings of pain in the dark.

It was during the long talks that Luisa learned that Elvita was knowledgeable about the drug trade and that she had gained this knowledge from people who frequented the Café Siempre. Elvita told her that there was much demand for marijuana in the United States. There was also a demand for heroin and cocaine, but it was the marijuana that was most popular, especially with students at the college in El Paso. The gringos always paid the going rate for the drug and the price was increasing every month. They had both seen the many well-dressed young Americans prowling the streets of Juarez looking for the weed.

Elvita was proud of the fact that her brother, Rogelio, worked for the organization that controlled the flow of all drugs into Ciudad Juarez and eventually across the river into El Paso. His boss thought of her brother as more of a son because Rogelio was his most honest and loyal pistolero. He was also very brave and had been wounded in a shoot-out with a rival who had tried to assassinate the boss.

Luisa had met Rogelio during one of his weekly visits to his sister. On each visit he brought his sister an envelope filled with money, and they often talked about another sister who had not spoken to or about Rogelio for years. The older sister had turned her back on him when she discovered that he was employed as a pistolero. She had called him her brother who was without shame. When Luisa met Rogelio on his first visit, he had asked her about her situation and she guardedly gave him some of the facts about her life and Club Azul. He began bringing her agua mineral and fresh fruit from the market near the bull ring. Her talks with him became the beginning of a trust that grew between them and she looked forward to his visits. She learned that he neither smoked nor drank and had ambitions of taking on more responsibility in the organization he worked for. He carried a silver pistol in his waistband and while they talked, he would take the gun out and place it near him, within easy reach.

Rogelio told her that it was known among his colleagues that her old boss Domingo made regular payments to a police comandante in Juarez. At times these payments amounted to very large sums of money which would be picked up by one of the comandante's men. Luisa remembered seeing the comandante visiting Domingo. Rogelio, in a very gentle and discreet way, offered to settle her affairs with Domingo. Luisa declined his offer, explaining that only the one whose honor was violated had the right of settling the affair. He smiled at her and she felt the bond between them grow, enough so that she began to gently probe into the details of the drug trade. She began to learn about the movement of the weed, its quality and value, and how to move shipments securely. Rogelio knew that she was prying into his business but he admired her courage and he trusted her, even though he sensed in her questions the possibility of something more than mere curiosity. So one day he asked her, in a direct manner, why she was so interested in the marijuana business. And she, being equally direct, told him. After listening to her plans and ideas, he saw, very clearly, an opportunity to offer his patron a new and cheaper source for this weed that was in such demand.

When she was alone in Elvita's apartment during the day with nothing to do but fight against the pain, she had begun to consider some possibilities that were idle thoughts at first. But as she felt her strength begin to flow back into her, the idle thoughts had turned into a plan.

In Luisa's small village in the Sierra her brother, Tomás, had inherited their father's natural gift for growing corn and vegetables in their small milpa outside the village. Her brother could get more corn out of the thin mountain soil than anyone for miles around. At the time of harvest she would help him take a share of the corn to the communal storage bin and after, they would take a wicker basket full of it to her mother and help her grind the corn for the masa which was the base for all their food. She remembered standing with her brother in the low scrub pines that bordered the hill just above the clearing beside a small stream several miles below their village. They had come to this clearing as children to trap rabbits that would feed on the grass next to the stream. But now the clearing was full of dark green plants that looked like large weeds. When she asked Tomás what it was he told her that it was marijuana and explained that it was like tobacco and people smoked it as one would tobacco, but that this weed made you feel like you did after drinking a few glasses of pulque. That was why people smoked it. She wanted to take some of the weed back to their uncle who liked pulque but Tomás told her that the men who grew this weed would kill them if they tried to steal it. He explained to her that the weed was worth much money and after it was harvested it would be taken to the large cities where it was transported to the gringos north of the Rio Bravo. Tomás had told her that the plants in the clearing were worth one hundred times more than one year's crop of corn.

She asked him why could they not grow it and he told her that a man from Casas Grandes controlled all the growing of it and that some Indians on the north side of the big barranca had tried to grow some but this man had them killed. The man was a renegade menonita who everyone called Piña because of his pockmarked face and he had many people working for him. Later that year when her mother took her and Tomás to market at Colonia Juarez to sell cornhusks, Tomás had pointed out this man to her. He was a thin man who dressed in very fine clothes and had a new pickup truck. But aside from that he looked like the other menonitas who came to market to sell their cheese.

Now, as each day passed into the next and her body healed, she began thinking of the other clearings and other streams south of the big barranca where this green weed could be grown. It would require money and connections but she had enough time to work on that.

She began thinking about Domingo's payments to the police comandante. Months ago, she had discovered that Domingo had a secret hiding place in his office. She had been passing by his office, and through the open door had seen him in a corner behind his desk on the floor. She moved closer to the door and saw a loose plank on the floor and a pile of wrist watches and gold necklaces and rings in a pile next to the plank. She did not know if he was putting something into or taking something out of the hole in the floor but did not have time to see because as he began to turn around, she quickly walked to the staircase and out of sight of his office.

———————————

During the next few weeks, Luisa made her plans to leave Ciudad Juarez and return to her village in the Sierra. She gave a good portion of her savings to Rogelio and asked him to give it to his sister, knowing that her friend would refuse it if offered in the manner of payment for the care and feeding she had provided to Luisa. She then went to the Mercado Central and bought a pair of jeans, a sweater, some sturdy boots, a heavy jacket, and a large bag made from an old serape which she could hang over her shoulder. She then began to walk to the Club Azul to settle matters with Domingo. She knew that the club would be deserted at this time of day and Domingo would, as was his habit, be taking his after-lunch siesta on one of the couches in the main lounge. And that is where she found him. He was stretched out on the sofa, sleeping peacefully. He was on his back, his handsome face was relaxed, and he had all the appearance of an innocent young boy. She watched for a few minutes so that she could be sure that he was deep in sleep and then she made her way up the stairs to his office. She went to the corner where she found the loose board and lifted it out of its place in the floor. Her eyes widened when she found several expensive looking watches, some gold jewelry, a large canvas sack, and a brown manila envelope. She opened the envelope and found several large bundles of cash. She took the cash out of the envelope and set it aside on the floor and pulled out the canvas sack. She tried to count the cash but it was too much for her and would take too much time. She calculated that there must be over ten thousand American dollars alongside a smaller pile of Mexican peso notes. She then took her old clothes out of her cloth bag and began placing the cash in the bag. She kept out most of the peso notes, which she stuffed into the front pockets of her new jeans. She opened the canvas bag and saw that it was full of five-peso coins. The bag weighed almost two kilos. She removed two hands full of coins and put them in her jacket pockets and silently walked over to the staircase where she could see Domingo, still asleep on the couch below.

Domingo was restless in his sleep, which Luisa knew was a sign that he would soon come awake. She grabbed the bag of coins by the top, raised it over her head and brought it down on Domingo's head. She did it again and again until she was sure that he was dead. She placed the bag of coins on his face. As she was leaving by the back door, she met one of the men who helped take care of the security of the club and whom she had often seen in the company of Domingo and the policeman they called the comandante. She nodded to him and when she got to the corner and looked back, she saw him holding the door open and looking at her.

———————•———————

It was mid-December and a cold wind came down the alley behind the club bringing small snowflakes from the west that cooled the scars on her face. She turned onto Avenida Juarez on her way south to the train depot. She moved with the crowd and panicked when she saw two uniformed police officers, but then relaxed when she realized that these men in the khaki uniforms were the policia municipal. She would be alert for the uniforms of policia judicial even though she knew they would not yet be aware of Domingo's death. Even when they learned of it, she doubted that their response would be very quick. The most concerned would be the comandante who had visited Domingo regularly. She felt the bulk of the American money in her bag, but planned to use the Mexican pesos to purchase her ticket. She pushed on the brass bars of the heavy, wooden doors of the train depot and felt the warmth of the interior chase away the sharpness of the cold and snow. She walked quickly to the bathrooms on the other side of the terminal. She closed the door to the stall and removed fifteen one-hundred-dollar bills from her bag. She removed her boots and placed five of the bills inside her stockings on each foot. She took five more bills and put them down the front of her jeans between her panties and bare stomach. She checked to make sure that her old clothes covered the cash in her bag and then walked out of the bathroom to the ticket counter.

The third-class compartment was crowded and she looked around for a vacant seat. She saw one near the center of the car and found herself sitting next to a priest who was absorbed in a book; he had red hair and very pale skin. He looked up when she sat down and moved over, closer to the window, so that she would have more space on the narrow wooden seat. He smiled at her.

"Good afternoon," he said.

"Good afternoon." She looked into his full blue eyes and then down at the book he was holding in his hands.

She held tightly to her bag. He had a very pleasant voice and she detected a strange accent. She would rather be sitting almost anywhere except next to a priest, but she believed in fate and this is where fate had placed her. Her mind was full of what she had done to Domingo and she feared that her concern must have been apparent to the priest. As soon as she had reached the safety of the train, she had felt a weakness in her resolve. Her hardened shell, tempered during her time at the club, had begun to soften. After all, to kill was to commit a mortal sin and she thought about the stain on her soul. You have committed other mortal sins, she told herself. Yes, she answered, but none so brutal.

The priest noticed the healing bruises on her face and the pink scars of the cuts. "All goes well?" he asked gently. His big, honest eyes looked at her.

"Oh, yes. Thank you for your concern. It is nothing. I was thinking about a friend." She lied. This priest knew something was out of place, and there was no human being more meddlesome than a priest when he sensed the need for intervention. She was, at least, grateful for the silence that followed her answer.

After a while, he asked, "Are you traveling far?"

"To Chihuahua, Father."

"I go there also." He noticed that she kept her eyes on the book and believing that she was curious, he held it up.

"Cervantes," he said. There was no acknowledgment or sign of recognition on her face and he realized that she might be illiterate.

"What is it about?" she asked.

"About a man seeking truth."

"How does he do that? How does he seek the truth?"

"Well, it is a novel. Fiction . . . ," he began.

"So it is not true?"

"Well, yes." The silence between them stayed for a moment.

"The author was not a particularly devout man but what I admire about him is that he recognized that man is born with an imperfect soul and gathers more imperfections as he lives and that it is only faith that removes these imperfections . . . ," he struggled to finish.

"I truly understand," she said.

"You have read Cervantes?"

"No. I read only the historietas. I like very much "Adelita" and "Libro Vaquero." She referred to the illustrated booklets sold by the millions in Mexico. They were a version of what the North Americans called comic books.

"May I know your name?"

"Lola. Lola Beltran," she lied and held out her hand.

"Like the singer?" he asked.

She shrugged. It was a small lie.

"I am Rodrigo De La Cruz. An appropriate name for a priest, no?"

"You are not Mexican?"

"No. I am Galician. From Spain."

"I am from the Sierra."

"I have spent time in the capital and two years in the Sierra Madre in Sonora among the Yaquis." He watched closely for her response.

"My great-grandfather was from there, but his family and many others were sent to the Yucatán by President Díaz."

"A tragedy," he said.

"No. An imperfection." She smiled at him.

They passed the miles across the great Chihuahuan Desert in talk about their families, their friends, the price of tortillas, and other general topics of their lives. She grew more comfortable with him because he spoke to her as a friend and not as a priest. He seemed genuinely curious about her life and her thoughts. She began to trust him a bit and then dared to explore the mysteries of the confession with him.

"Is it enough to admit your sins to yourself and then punish yourself for committing them?" she asked.

"No. The church requires that confessions be made to a priest," he told her.

"In a confessional? In a church?" she asked.

"Well, not always. Yes, sometimes outside the church."

"So, it is not enough to admit them to yourself. Like in the song?"

"Song?" he asked.

"Yes." She repeated the words from the old song: "En el frío de la noche, castiga la alma y pierdes la fe."

"I have never heard that song." His interest increased. She was full of surprises.

"It is an old Mexican song. I learned it many years ago."

"How is it called?"

"'Amor de la Calle,'" she said.

"No, Lola. No matter how cold the night, God does not want you to punish your soul and he certainly does not want you to lose your faith. God himself does not want to punish your soul, he wants to forgive it. But he can only do this if you confess your sins to him. And I ask you, not as a priest, but as a new friend, please do not lose your faith."

They were silent for a long time as the train passed through the darkness of northern Mexico. A weariness overcame her and she fought off sleep. She had much to think about and she wanted to do it before she fell asleep, but she could not stop thinking about what this priest told her. He was different; he had made her consider the possibility of confessing to him and relieving the burden she felt. His questions were not probing. His words were like small caresses. True caresses. Not like those bought at the Club Azul. Those were always temporary, meaningless, lasting only the period of time for which they were bought. She planned to start again but without imperfections. Could she do that without confessing? She longed for the comfort she had felt as a young girl at the small church in the Sierra. But she had forsaken that comfort long ago and had not thought about it for years. She had shut out her former life and had accepted her life up north as fate. Nothing more. She rubbed the back of her neck and felt the scab that had formed over the cut where Domingo had kicked her. It was dry and hard and some of her hair was stuck in it. She was afraid to rub it because it would start bleeding again. Finally, she could no longer keep her eyes open, so she leaned her head back against the seat and fell asleep.

The priest watched her as she slept. How stupid of me not to have seen! he thought. The bruises and the cuts stood out in the peacefulness of sleep. He should have known but he had not been listening closely enough, prattling on about Cervantes in his ego and pride of knowledge. Many of her profession had passed through his confessional. He had seen them at Mass on countless Sundays and now remembered the deep sadness he had felt. The sadness and hopelessness that had at times worn him down and made him question his own faith. He had done his priestly duties: taken their confession, assigned them penance, and served them communion. He had never talked with them as he had this one. This Lola, which he had accepted was not her true name, was the first. Perhaps, he thought, she had more strength than he.

———————

Comandante Mondragón of the Chihuahua State Judicial Police sipped his coffee and watched the passengers in the central train station. His investigator's eye noticed the contrast in the controlled desperation of the country people and the bored acceptance of this swirl of humanity on the faces of the businessmen. It had been more than a year since he'd had anything to do with trains. He was here only because his counterpart in Ciudad Juarez had asked him, as a favor, to handle this matter personally. He stirred his coffee and looked over to the entrance of the small bistro where two of his men stood and watched the crowd. The comandante in Juarez had given Mondragón a complete description of a young Indian woman and how she was dressed. She would be on the Juarez to Chihuahua train. He had explained the circumstances of her crime—the killing of a pimp who was a top informant in the border city. Mondragón would have normally assigned this matter to his subordinate and would not have been personally involved. But he could not ignore the favor asked of him by a fellow comandante, who told him that the woman would have in her possession a large amount of money. Mondragón knew the request was because this young Indian woman took the money from the pimp after she killed him and that the money was part of an arrangement between his colleague and the pimp. The Juarez train was not due for a quarter of an hour. He signaled the waiter for another coffee and begin to think back to his meeting earlier this morning.

There had been no need for introductions; they were both well known in the city. The man sitting across the table from him was a prominent banker from one of the largest banks in the north. The banker spoke in the language of a politician; indirect and imprecise with no specific details of any proposed arrangements. This irritated the comandante, who was more comfortable with the clear and concise language of his profession, but then he understood that the purpose of this meeting was not to discuss any detail of a proposal but to establish whether he, the comandante, would be open to a business arrangement. The details would only come if and when he agreed. The banker presented several key hypothetical scenarios, never once indicating that he was connected to the principals of the business in question. He referred to central distribution sites for commodities not unlike that of stockyards, where the cattle of northern Chihuahua were gathered near railroad spurs for shipping to various destinations.

Comandante Mondragón recognized the danger of asking any question that would lead to discussion of the plans of the principals to which the banker alluded. The fact that he had been chosen as a man who could be of assistance troubled him. If he agreed there would be, no doubt, a very large stream of money coming his way, but he knew there would be more demands and more involvement in the future of this enterprise, which would put a target on his back. He would become rich, but the chances of him living long enough to enjoy it would narrow with his continued participation. He knew that the proposal would be for access to remote areas of his jurisdiction which would serve as locations for airstrips and facilities to move marijuana and other drugs across the border to the gringos. He was already aware of small operations that brought the marijuana from the Sierra to locations in the north for transshipment, and there was more demand from the gringos for the Mexican heroin which came from farther south in the republic. If he became a part of this, his life would change forever. His reputation as a man of integrity would be gone. His life would also change if he did not agree. He would be swept aside by those who would gladly accept this proposal after he rejected it. At best, he would be dismissed from his position; but it was more likely that he would be dead in a very short time.

As the new comandante, he had dismissed the corrupt officers and brought on board a group of men who shared his vision of the laws of the republic and the enforcement of those laws. Like all comandantes he received a very small budget. It was nowhere near enough to cover the cost of equipment, facilities, training, or the salaries for himself and his men. And like all the other comandantes, he was expected to pay for his operations through the seizures of money and property of the criminals he brought to justice or through the bribes from the people who would benefit from him turning a blind eye to their activities. A portion of his income would also make its way up the chain to those who were responsible for him maintaining his position. It was like an army living off the land. The largest seizures were from the gangs in the growing drug trade. Cash, good vehicles, and weapons were plentiful. If he should accept the coming offer, he would have enough money to pay his men, provide them with good equipment, training, and modern weapons. But to what purpose? He and his men would only become like those whom they now pursued.

There was a strong rumor that a new agency was being created by the incoming president of the republic whose campaign promise was to stamp out corruption in the military and law enforcement. Agencies like this had been created in the past, lasted a while, and then faded away; and when they did, the criminal element became stronger and more organized. Every time these new agencies were created they took more from the national and state budgets for agencies like his, and in the end corruption was never addressed. So he told the banker the only thing he could and that was that he would consider further discussions and would give him an answer soon. The banker had proposed another meeting in one week.

His men spotted the girl as she got off the train. She was walking with and talking to a priest. Mondragón and his men followed the girl and the priest out of the station and down several streets where they both went into a café. Mondragón sent his men inside to see that the girl did not try to leave by the rear exit. He noticed that she was very petite and could not have weighed more than fifty kilos. She was dark and definitely Indian and so he was surprised by her continual conversation with the priest. Indians were known for their reluctance to speak much, especially with non-Indians. Well, he thought, I will give her a chance to talk with me when she comes out of the café.

Luisa saw the three men waiting for her as she stepped out onto the sidewalk. The tall one was, without a doubt, in charge. He wore a dark suit and a white shirt with no tie and she noticed the polished Western boots as he stood slightly behind the other two. He looked like her favorite movie star, Jorge Negrete. He had the same neatly trimmed mustache and the same kind eyes with the burden of the world reflected in them.

"Momento, señorita." He had a calm voice and he ignored the priest as his two men moved to either side of Luisa. One who had hard eyes put his hand on her bag. Only after the one in charge was satisfied that Luisa would not try to run did he turn his attention to the priest.

"Excuse us, Father, but I have business with the señorita. I am Comandante Mondragón of the State Judicial Police and I would like to ask a few questions and then you are free to go." He turned to Luisa. "You are Luisa Jurado Hernandez?"

"Yes." She knew it was all over and that the comandante knew everything. It would serve for nothing to lie. The prospect of being taken to prison made her knees tremble.

The comandante turned back to the priest. "My sergeant will stay with you while we talk with the señorita." The larger of the two men moved over to the priest. Luisa went with the comandante and the other policeman to the mouth of a small alley two doors down from the café.

"There is no need for an interrogation, is there?" he asked.

"No, mi comandante. It will serve for nothing." She handed her bag over to him.

Mondragón felt inside the bag and found the loose cash at the bottom under the old clothes. After removing the cash, he replaced the clothes and handed her bag to her. He then slowly counted out the cash. Luisa felt the fear rise in her as she thought of the money in her boots and inside the front of her panties but she decided she would not volunteer any cooperation.

Mondragón studied her very closely, taking in the large amount of damage done to her face. He had not seen that much damage done unless the face belonged to a body in the morgue. His colleague in Juarez was evasive when Mondragón asked him about a warrant from the prosecutor for the girl. This meant only one thing. His colleague would send some men for the girl and she would disappear. This pimp, he thought, deserved his fate and he felt a bit of admiration for the small waif standing in front of him. He would return most of the cash to the comandante in Juarez, but he would be damned if he would take the little one into custody. There was no legal demand for her arrest so he had had no problem with letting her go.

"Mira señorita, there is no interest in taking you in. The only interest is to recover the missing money and we have done so. Do you understand me?" He looked closely at the bruises and the fresh scars on her face. Luisa, who appreciated his formality, nodded, not quite believing him.

"Where were you going?" he asked.

"Muy lejos de aqui."

"Yes, clearly you must be far away from here, and soon. I do not mean to threaten, but if you are found in or even near Chihuahua City after tonight, things will only get worse for you. In truth, the worst. Do you understand me?"

She nodded, looking at him with her honest eyes standing out from the wounds on her face and then asked, "Un favor?"

"Yes, if it is possible," he smiled.

"I have no money other than that," she nodded toward the cash in his hand, "and if I had three hundred dollars, it would help me get far away."

"Ay, que huevos!" the short policeman standing next to her laughed.

The comandante smiled, "I think one hundred will serve just as well." He handed her a one-hundred-dollar bill and made a mental note to subtract that amount from his counterpart's cut.

Luisa stuffed the folded bill in the front pocket of her jeans and as she put her old clothes back in the bag, she felt the other bills crisp and warm on her belly.

"May I say goodbye to Father de la Cruz?" she asked.

"Of course."

After the priest said goodbye and gave her a blessing, he watched her hurry down the street in the direction of the bus station. Then he and the comandante walked back to the trains.

"The Señorita Jurado is not a criminal, Father, but she got caught up with some bad people recently. These bad ones robbed a bank several days ago and talked her into holding some of the loot. Very sad."

"Was it them that beat her?" the priest asked.

"Without a doubt. These people are without honor or scruples."

The priest felt better about things and about Luisa, especially after he saw the policeman give her some money. Perhaps there is some decency in these city people, he thought.

They stopped in front of the newsstands inside the terminal.

"Buen viaje, padre," the comandante nodded.

"Vaya con Dios, señor." The priest made the sign of the cross. He bought one local and two of the national daily newspapers at the kiosk. Later, as the train rolled past the southern edges of Chihuahua City and the scattered buildings gave way to the large empty spaces of the desert, he searched each newspaper carefully but was disappointed that there was not a word about any bank robbery in this part of Mexico.

Luisa boarded a bus with the other passengers and looked for a seat in the back, away from the others. She sat quietly and looked out into the dusk of the foothills. Darkness came quickly on the eastern slope of the Sierra. Passengers began to file down the aisle, filling all the seats. All of them were from the Sierra and they reminded her of the family she had left behind. They all seemed to carry worn cardboard boxes, large cloth bags, or babies. The bus was already thirty minutes behind schedule, but she fell into that familiarity with the fact that in the Sierra time moved at a different pace. An older woman pushing a young boy of six or seven years ahead of her sat down next to Luisa. She directed the boy into the seats across the aisle. The boy was followed by a younger woman carrying an infant. This woman also carried a cardboard box and two bags slung over her shoulder. After they stowed their belongings, the older woman adjusted her clothes and without a word she held a newspaper cone filled with chicharrónes out to Luisa. Luisa thanked her in their language, took one, put it in her mouth and bit into the fried bit of pork skin. The fat, savory taste of the rind, made more flavorful by the sauce of the chile de árbol, filled her with comfortable memories and she had to remind herself not to let her guard down.

Her mind was already back in her village with her brother and the sixteen hundred American dollars which was the small fortune that would fund the beginning of their new business. She already knew the perfect place for growing the weed. Now she would need to establish protected routes into and out of this area, plan delivery to Rogelio's people, and have a plan of action to deal with Piña and his people. She would also need to establish some sort of protection from the authorities and, at a later date, she would approach the handsome comandante with the kind eyes in Chihuahua City and try to make an arrangement. As for Piña, there was no doubt that he and his associates would view Luisa's operation as a serious threat. She knew the workers who tended his crops in the Sierra were of her people and, like her people, they distrusted those who were not from the Sierra, especially the menonitas. The workers would not present a problem, in fact, they would be of much assistance when the time came to take over Piña's fields. As for Piña, well, he was just another man and she could deal with him in the same manner that she had dealt with Domingo.

She sat back in her seat and looked out the window into the darkness of the foothills and heard the increasing whine of the bus engine as the driver downshifted for the climb into the high Sierra. There were many preparations to be made. So much to do with so little time because the season for planting would be here before she knew it.

The bus dropped her and several other women at the front of the small store in the village that served as the terminal for passengers. A small light stood out from the top of the store and spread a circle of light that did not quite reach the road. The other passengers, laden with their bags of goods, slipped out of the light and faded into the darkness of the village. Luisa stood there for a while watching the snow come down lightly in the circle of light. It was colder at this altitude and the snowflakes seemed smaller, even thinner here, and she hardly noticed them as they melted on her face. She looked around in the light, then she too moved out of the light and walked out of the village, north in the direction of her brother's small milpa. Out in the open it was colder, and as she moved away from the village, the surrounding hills and outlying buildings appeared as dark images that returned to her memory as familiar landmarks. The chill of the mountain air reminded her of the moment she had walked out of the Club Azul after killing Domingo. Now that she was back in the Sierra, the guilt of her mortal sin began to diminish and only a small regret remained that Domingo's death would never restore all of the honor he had stolen from her. But, she admitted to herself, her mortal sin guaranteed that he would never again be able to take even the tiniest bit of honor from her or anyone else. She walked on through the cold and her steps were lighter now, gliding over the dirt path while she wondered if that might make her sin less serious. In a little while she saw the outline of her brother's house at the edge of the shadow of the surrounding hills and she felt the comfort one feels upon returning home. She thought about the priest and how he had pleaded for her to not lose her faith and told her about the importance of confession. She wished that she would now be able to tell him that he should not concern himself about that. She would find a church and a priest far away from the Sierra and would confess her sins. It would have to be done when she could travel to such a place but there was time for that later. Besides, she thought, there was a small realization beginning to take place in her that there might be additional things to confess to in the future.

THE ART OF LIFE

The storm ended the Friday Night Fights before the bell rang to start the first round. As the clouds formed high over the small town, the electricity in them broke up the radio signals and covered the voice of the announcer. Nothing but static with occasional bursts of a high, tinny shriek came out of the brown plastic grill of the radio that sat on a shelf above the toasters in the small kitchen of the Desert Rose Café. It was past closing time and Ruth had already cleaned the large grill of the cast iron stove, turned off the burners, and was looking forward to hearing the fights over a cup of coffee and a cigarette. Etienne, the deputy sheriff, reached up and switched off the radio.

"Damn shame! That new kid, Clay, was fighting tonight." He put his empty coffee cup on the shelf next to the sink. The deputy had boxed as a light heavyweight in the Third

Fleet championship finals during his time in the Pacific and he enjoyed listening to the radio broadcast of the Friday night fights with Ruth and her husband, Henry.

Lightning flashed and lit up the kitchen. Ruth stood still, waiting, counting silently to herself. In a few seconds the crash of thunder filled the small kitchen.

"Gettin' closer," she said.

With no fight to take up part of the evening, she walked through the batwing doors into the dining room of the café to start cleaning up for the night. As the deputy followed her out of the kitchen, the rain began.

"I better start my rounds of the saloons." He reached over to the rack on the wall and grabbed his hat. He listened as the intensity of the rain increased. It was pouring heavily onto the roof of the café.

"Too early for any trouble, ain't it?"

"You never know." The deputy walked over to the front door.

He had just put on his hat when the door opened and two small girls quickly slipped through the open space. Etienne reached behind them and shut the door. He looked at the girls. The little one held her older sister's hand and they both shivered in the cold air. Their hair was matted from the rain and the wetness rolled off them in a stream that formed a puddle around their bare feet. Ruth came over from behind the counter.

"What are y'all doin' out in this rain? Where's your mama?"

"She said she had to go shoppin', Miss Ruth." The older one said. She did not appear intimidated by the tone of Ruth's question.

Ruth and the deputy exchanged a quick look. The girls kept their eyes on Ruth. They always reminded the deputy of a couple of mistreated puppies. The youngest, Mandy, was five years old and her sister, Abigail, was eight. They shared the same disheveled appearance and the same classic beauty of their mother, DeeAnne. The mother was the problem, he thought. She was one of those rare beauties, hell-bent on her own destruction. He had seen others like her in his time and they had all eventually reached their goal, always leaving a flaming wreck behind them. Everyone in the small town who knew them agreed that these young girls deserved better. Ruth went back into the kitchen and fired up the right side of the grill and then came back into the dining area.

"You girls hungry?" The anger had gone out of her voice.

"Yes, ma'am," the oldest answered. The young one remained silent.

"All right, then. We'll fix up some grilled cheese sandwiches, but first y'all gotta go into the ladies' room and wash your hands." She inspected them closely. "And your faces too. And don't you be leavin' a mess in there either!"

"We won't, Miss Ruth."

Thunder shook the room and lightning flashed, ricocheting off the chrome face of the milk dispenser. The young one flinched and moved closer to her sister. They went into the bathroom and the older one turned on the lights.

"I'll go check the bars, see if I can find her."

"She's probably gone off to El Paso with one of her beaus." Ruth looked around, afraid the girls might hear her. "Damn it, Etienne! This is gettin' out of hand. They're like a couple of stray cats. They know I'll feed 'em and give 'em a place to stay, so they keep comin' back. It can't go on like this. Henry's giving me hell for bringin' them home. But then, what else can I do?" She poured out two glasses of milk and put them on a table.

"Last week I met with a couple of the church people who would like to take them in, but legally, nothing can be done without Dee's consent."

"There ought to be a better way."

The deputy shrugged. "I'd best be going."

"I'm locking up. When you come back, come through the kitchen door."

The girls came out of the bathroom. Abigail had combed their hair out with her fingers. The young one did not look up but she appeared to be less frightened.

"I want you girls to spend the night at my place. No need going back to the apartment if your mama's not going to be there." It made her feel good when the girls both broke out in smiles.

"Miss Ruth, can we have dodgers and sop for breakfast?"

"Biscuits and gravy is what you mean to say, Abigail. I will not have y'all talking like ranch hands nor eating like them either. That stuff will make you fat."

"But why Miss Ruth? Ranch hands eat dodgers—I mean, biscuits and gravy—all the time and they don't get fat."

"They don't get fat because they work it off. They work real hard."

"DeeAnne says that hard work is for eejits." The smallest spoke up. "What's an eejit, Miss Ruth?"

"It's something your mama knows a lot about. Now, y'all come with me into the kitchen and help with the sandwiches."

Later, Ruth watched them as they ate. She had cut their sandwiches into four pieces and stood the pieces on end, circling a few potato chips and presenting the plain grilled cheese sandwiches in as elegant a manner as possible. She had been teaching the girls proper manners and had instructed them in the way decent people behaved at the table. The first time she fed them they had held their forks in their small fists with the handle sticking out of the top of their hands, next to the thumb. She remembered them eating like feral cats, hunched over their food, arms on the table on either side of their plates and looking around as they shoveled food into their mouths. They had eaten quickly, like they were expecting someone to take the food away before they could finish.

So she watched proudly as they sat with their backs straight, one hand in their laps, and taking small, delicate bites from their quartered sandwiches. After taking a bite they would put the uneaten portion back on their plates and touch their mouths with the paper napkins Ruth laid out next to their plates. They had come a long way and she was proud of them. She could still not get the younger one to speak very much, but she would work on that. She was happy with her decision to take the girls home with her tonight and fully expected Henry to grumble about it. He was about as sensitive as the D-7 Caterpillar he drove, but he was essentially a kind soul. She sensed he was fearful of becoming too attached to the girls because she often found him fussing over them in his gruff way. She watched them eat and knew full well that she had no solution to the circumstances of their lives. She had thought of approaching DeeAnne and trying to reason with her but had not because she knew it was hopeless. Dee had once worked for her at the café and they had gotten along well until Ruth discovered that Dee was helping herself to money from the cash register on a regular basis. On the day Ruth fired her, DeeAnne had let loose a barrage of curse words that got the attention of several ranch hands who were eating lunch in the café. At the time, Ruth remembered being frightened by the look of pure anger in DeeAnne's face. She tried to think kindly of Dee but she held no doubt that the woman would cause trouble for her at every opportunity. She had made her mind up that she would not send the girls back to the little hovel of an apartment they lived in on this night because if Etienne was successful in finding Dee she'd be too drunk to look after the girls.

It was a cold rain. One of those storms that come in the early spring and at times will bring hail. This storm came before the planting of the crops and now even if it brought hail there would be no damage to the farms. If it had come early next month then it would have ruined some of the newly planted crops. Timing and balance, Etienne thought, a fragile line that separated a good cleaning rain from a near disaster. The heavy rain flowed down the windshield of his pickup truck as he sat in it at the front of his small office squeezed between the barber's and the radio repair shop on Main Street. He watched the rain pour down onto the hood of his truck. It was a liquid sheet that blurred the lettering and the large badge painted on the window of his office. He had not found Dee in any of the bars in town. Nobody had seen her tonight. If Dee had gone into El Paso, there was a good chance she would end up in jail again. She had been arrested three times in the last six months; twice for drunk and disorderly and once for aggravated assault on a police officer. She had been given suspended sentences because the public defender made a very good case for her not being taken away from her children, but eventually the courts would lose patience and she would be put behind bars. The county would then take her kids from her and place them in a county facility. If Dee-Anne was sentenced to more than thirty days, the girls would be placed in foster homes and the deputy knew that it was unlikely that they would be placed in the same home. They would be assigned to different families and although the system would do its best to keep them close, Mandy, the youngest, would not react well to being separated from her sister. The senselessness of it all filled him with frustration. It was clear that DeeAnne was headed for disaster and she was taking the two kids with her. A radio call brought him out of his thoughts. It was the night dispatcher.

"Etienne? Are you there?"

He grabbed the microphone. "Yes, Jo, I read you five-by."

"Landline the sheriff A-S-A-P. He has something for you.

"Ten-four!"

Etienne got out of his truck and walked to his office and dialed headquarters.

"Hey, Sheriff, it's Etienne."

"Howdy, Etienne. DeeAnne Palmer. You know her?

"Yep. I'm out looking for her now."

"Well, I can tell you where to find her. She's at County General in El Paso. She was cut up pretty bad in a knife fight."

"She gonna make it?"

"Yeah, looks like it, but that ain't her main problem. The woman she was fighting with is DOA. Seems like this DeeAnne woman stabbed her in the heart. A bar full of witnesses, so it's gonna be an easy one for the DA. Why were you looking for her?"

"She's left her kids alone again."

"Well, they won't be alone long. Their mama ain't coming home, so the county will take them until some kind of foster arrangement can be made."

"Sheriff, I need to talk to you about that." Etienne took off his hat and sat in the wooden chair behind his desk. He then explained the girls' situation and made several suggestions that would delay any action by the county for at least a week or two.

After he hung up the phone, he sat there thinking hard but was not able to come up with a plan for the girls. He knew he had to get over to Ruth's and tell her about DeeAnne. He locked up his office, got in his pickup, and thinking angry thoughts about the selfishness of the girl's mother, he drove through the rain back to the Desert Rose Café.

The girls finished their meal and Ruth watched as they cleared the table and washed their dishes in the big galvanized steel sink in the back. If I had enough time with them, I would see that they had the proper upbringing and education, she thought. I could take them to church with me on Sunday where they could learn about the love of Jesus and I could teach them about the good things in life. It would be a struggle, she thought, but worth it.

Years ago, Etienne had told her about somebody in ancient history; she thought it may have been an emperor but wasn't sure. This man, whoever he was, said: "Life is more akin to the art of wrestling than the art of dancing." The quote had stuck with her. The way the deputy said it was crystal clear and elegant. Etienne read a lot of books and often quoted great people of history. She could not remember the other quotes but she remembered this one because she believed in it. It was the way she had always lived. She had wrestled with life and never once even thought of trying to dance around it. And this situation with the girls? Yes, she thought, I'll wrestle this too.

She was beginning to feel better about things and had regained some of her hope when the deputy came in through the kitchen. Ruth was helping the girls with a jigsaw puzzle she had laid out on a table as they waited for Henry, who was on his way back from El Paso. The younger one, who had been chatting away, shut up when the deputy appeared. Ruth looked at the deputy and then back at Mandy. Then it dawned on her that the little one was afraid of men. Dear Lord, Ruth thought, no! DeeAnne was always dragging all kinds of men home with her; and as she thought about this, the dark images began to form in her mind and she felt a chill run through her. She forced the thoughts from her mind and thought, I'll deal with this later. I don't want Etienne to know my thinking on this until I can find out more. So she shut out her bad ideas and went over to the deputy who stood behind the counter near the coffee urn. He had removed his hat and he looked a little bit lost.

"You want a cup of coffee?" she asked.

"I'd rather have a small glass of buttermilk."

As she poured the buttermilk, she looked up at him with her questions written on her face. Speaking in a quiet voice he told Ruth about Dee Anne. Ruth stood between him and the girls. She showed no emotion but did feel a sense of relief when Etienne told her about the sheriff willing to intercede with Child Protective Services and try to arrange some type of temporary foster arrangements so that the girls would not have to be relocated.

"The sheriff's got a lot of pull, but he told me that whoever wanted to take the girls in had to be certified by the state." He sipped at the buttermilk. It eased the burning in his stomach.

"Henry and I thought about adopting years ago. It's probably a lot like that."

"I don't know much about it, but I can call some people I know and I can get back to the church people."

They were both quiet, listening to the girls chatter over the jigsaw puzzle. Etienne felt better about things when he saw the spark in Ruth's eye and the determined set of her jaw. There might just be enough horsepower between them to make this work, he thought. He finished the buttermilk and put down the empty glass.

He nodded toward the girls who were engrossed in the puzzle.

"Do you need anything?"

"No. Everything is good. I'm taking them home with me tonight."

"OK." He put some coins near the cash register. "I'll be goin' then. Who's fighting next Friday night?"

"Don't know, but Henry'll be bringing the El Paso papers home with him. I'll let you know tomorrow." She picked up the coins and rang the charge up on the cash register.

"All right then. See you tomorrow."

"Good night." She followed behind him and locked the door.

The rain had stopped and the clean smell of the desert that always followed a good rain washed over him as he got into his pickup truck. He knew that tomorrow, with the warmth of the morning sun, the valley floor would begin anew. The dust would be washed off the creosote bush, increasing the power of its scent. The ocotillos would begin to grow a green beard on their spiny stalks and in a few weeks the bright orange-red flowers would bloom at the very top. The petals would attract bees, hummingbirds, and the occasional passing mounted ranch hand who would pluck the petals, put them in his mouth, and enjoy the sweetness of their nectar.

In a country that was lucky to see ten inches of rain in a year, the rain's magic brought out the best in the plant life of the desert. It was an occasion that always got the deputy's attention. As he pulled up to the stop sign at the town's main street, he noticed the red light flashing on the pole above the Broken Spur Saloon, which told him that there was trouble inside. People misbehaving on a late Friday evening, he thought, not wanting to miss the opportunity for a good brawl before closing time.

He drove into the parking lot in front of the saloon and got out of his truck. He pulled on a pair of tight fitting, tan leather work gloves and cinched the straps down tight. As he walked through the fresh, clean air to the trouble that waited for him behind the tall wooden doors of the saloon, he thought of DeeAnne in the prison ward of the county hospital and how it was a damn shame that the rain's magic didn't work on all of God's creatures.

GOLLY GLOVES

I t was a small arena without pretense because it was built by people without pretense. There were no seat backs, no grandstands, no private boxes, only rows of planked lumber from the bottom to the top where a railing, three boards high, served as a concession to safety for small children and drinking adults. The only covered structure was the announcer's booth, which was built over the top row of seats in the middle of the west side. The announcers had a commanding view of the whole arena floor from the pens in the north end to the south end where several railroad ties served as anchors for a solid wall of wood. There were two large army surplus speakers on top of the booth, their original olive drab faded to a dull gray-green with freckles of rust. Only one of them worked. There was a set price for seats except for those in the north end which were closest to the stock pens. When the wind was out of the north it brought with it the heavy aroma of cow manure and the flies that thrived in it. These seats were sold at a two-dollar discount.

Peggy and her sister had tickets for these seats, halfway up from the arena floor. The younger girl, Judy, would turn eighteen tomorrow and the tickets were a birthday gift from her older sister. To their immediate left, the fence of the cattle chutes ran the entire width of the arena and in the middle, there was a wooden gate whose wheels fit onto a long piece of heavily greased angle iron on which the gate slid open and closed.

Peggy watched the bull rider as he sat on the top rail of the holding pen. He was studying the bull who was pushing against the restraining wood of the enclosure. The girls could hear the clanging of the bell tied onto the bull with a rope that ran over his back to his chest. The cowboy reminded Peggy of the television cowboy who advertised cigarettes. He was older than the other contestants, and was dressed in the usual rodeo getup; a hat, Western-style shirt with snap buttons, jeans worn under chaps, and boots with small-roweled spurs. She noticed a mended tear in the cowboy's shirt below the pocket on the right side and that his hat was a bit crumpled and worn and stained through at the band.

She watched the rider tap the crown of his hat with his open hand, pushing it down on his head until the tops of his ears bent down slightly. Then, he slid quickly onto the top of the bull and wrapped his gloved left hand in the rope attached to the one that ran around the bull's girth, pulled up several times and took another wrap of the rope, and patted the wrap with his right hand. He spoke a few words to the cowboy at the head of the holding pen who spoke to the young cowboy on the arena floor who quickly slid the gate open. Peggy could feel the angry explosion of the bull who, freed from his tormentors, now tried to rid himself of the human on his back. He flew sideways into the arena and jumped into the air, thrusting his rear legs up and out. His front legs slammed into the turf of the arena floor and he twisted his massive body, trying to throw the cowboy who was holding onto the rope with only his left hand. The cowboy's right hand was out at right angles to his body, then up above his head, then down at his side. He gripped the bull's sides with his thighs, trying to maintain his balance and stay on the pitching beast.

Peggy watched him closely. He did not grimace or clamp his teeth like the younger riders. He seemed to calculate the moves of the bull and measure his own responses. She could see the bull's powerful neck as he thrust his horns this way and that, his eyes rolling desperately in their sockets, his hooves hitting the ground again and again, his eyes now full of anger and hate for the rider who was hurting him with his spurs.

The bull threw the cowboy before the official's horn sounded at the eight-second mark. The rider fell to the ground on the right side of the pitching bull. The bull ran on for a couple of feet and then turned to his left, made a full circle, and faced the cowboy who was on his back in the churned earth of the arena floor. As the bull lowered his head to begin his charge, the cowboy stood up, grabbed his hat from the ground and moved in a quick, graceful sidestep and the bull's short horns cut close to the man but found only air. The rider watched the bull, a frown on his face. The rodeo clowns taunted the bull and he chased them to the gate that led to the stock chutes. The rider stood in the middle of the arena with his hat now back on his head and yelled at the bull:

"Come back here you sorry son of a bitch, I ain't through with you!" He then walked slowly back to the gate that had unleashed him and the bull into the arena.

"His name is Pete Pickford, from San Angelo, Texas, and he is making my little heart go pitter patter!" Judy was reading his name from the faded mimeographed sheets of the program. Peggy smiled at her sister. Judy was still young and did not have a clue about the game played between a woman and a man. Peggy had tried to tell her about some of the pitfalls when it came to men but her younger sister ignored her advice. Peggy kept her eye on the cowboy, remembering the look on his face after he was thrown. It was a look of determination, and it told Peggy that he knew that he had not completed his task. He had only run out of time. It told her that the bull might have won this round, but that there would be other rounds to come. The cowboy was not even close to being defeated. No, she thought, this man did not know how to quit. Of this, she was quite certain, for she had definitely had her share of quitters.

At seven o'clock that evening, Peggy watched the bull rider walk into the Pronghorn Saloon. He moved with the painful grace of a rodeo veteran whose self-confidence was just short of arrogance. He caught her look and smiled at her. She felt a slight rush as she went back to work on a faulty beer tap in front of the mirrored back bar. She was helping out on the evening shift during rodeo week and the owner, knowing her mechanical skills, had asked her to fix the clogged beer lines. As she removed a cracked and slimy hose, she thought about the bull rider, Pete. She couldn't remember his last name. She noticed that he had removed his hat as soon as he had entered the saloon. This marked him as a man with some manners, since all the young cowboys and those who dressed as cowboys refused to remove their hats for any reason. They even wore them at the table while they ate. She watched Pete sit down at the far end of the bar. He sat alone, not speaking with anyone. He did not have the look of concentration that Peggy saw in the arena that afternoon. His eyes held a sparkle, a glint of mischief.

It was almost ten, close to the end of her shift before she worked her way to Pete's end of the bar. He had a five-drink look on his face and seemed to be staring at the bottles on the back bar.

"I saw you ride today."

The words came to him through the whiskey without any meaning, but his muddled mind did register a pleasant, soft voice. He moved his eyes in the direction of that voice. She was blond. Pretty. Smiling.

"Huh?" A croak was all he could manage. He ran his tongue over his gums looking for moisture.

"Sorry," he recovered, "you caught me deep in thought."

"You want some water to chase that whiskey?" she smiled.

"Yes, thank you." She walked to the other end of the bar, past the sinks, and pulled one of the tap handles, which poured out a glass full of clear water.

"I didn't mean to bother you but I did see you ride today."
She put the glass of water in front of him. He drank off half
of it.

"How much of the event did you see?"

"Just the bull riding."

"You mean, you saw me get thrown." His headache returned.

"Yes!"

"It was definitely not my day!" He winced as the pain increased.
He had some aspirin out in the truck but he did not want to
break off talking with this pretty blonde. "My name is Pete." He
held out his hand.

"Peggy." She shook his hand. "Glad to know you." She took
a small bottle of aspirin out of her apron pocket and placed it
on the bar next to his glass of water. "Do you only ride bulls?"

"No, I do some bulldogging and roping," he lied. Since he
had hurt his back two years ago at the Cow Palace, he no longer
even thought of putting up money for those events. The back
brace he was forced to wear while competing limited the mobility needed for 'dogging and roping.

"You going to ride tomorrow?"

"I'll know in the morning." He took some tablets from the
bottle and slid it back across the bar towards her. He took an
immediate liking to her and it wasn't just the whiskey. There
was a kindness about her, like she was not afraid of dealing
with other people's worries. He saw the small lines at the cor-
ners of her eyes and a long thin scar that ran from the edge of
her lower lip to her chin. They talked about the town, the
state's Triple-A baseball team, the new interstate highway that
would soon replace old Route 66, and other things of everyday

life. She was friendly and witty and talking with her relaxed him and pushed away the tension that always came with the anticipation of driving to another event hundreds of miles away, on little or no sleep. Shortly after ten o'clock she reached behind her and untied her apron.

"My shift is over. You want another drink before I leave?"

"No. I'm fine." He looked at the fake Rolex on his left wrist. "Ten o'clock. Kind of early isn't it?"

"I'm only working fill-in during rodeo week. Five to ten."

"Can I give you a ride?"

"Thanks, but no. My car is outside."

"You working tomorrow night?"

"Yep, all week." She folded the apron.

"How about tomorrow—"

"Look, Pete," she cut him off. "No offense, but I'm going to pick up my kid from my sister and then I'm going to get some sleep so I can get up early, take my kid back to my sister's place, and then work the breakfast shift over at the Little Diner. I don't have a hell of a lot of spare time." She smiled at him.

"No offense taken," he smiled. "Well, how about I get tickets to the big show on Saturday for you and the kid? Can you get the day off?"

She finished folding the apron and put it beneath the bar. She did not want to tell him that the same offer was made to her by two saddle bronc riders, a roper, and one of the rodeo managers. And she could never bring herself to tell him about trying to get her child into the School for the Deaf over in Santa Fe. She was not bitter about what life had handed her but she did not see how a rodeo rider full of whiskey could be of any help. In a day or two, he would be gone and she was sorry about that. She would like nothing better than to get to know him. She liked his easy, open manner and his honest eyes. And, she thought, most importantly, he did not talk about himself.

"I appreciate the offer, but I just don't have the time," she smiled.

"That's OK, maybe I'll see you tomorrow."

He watched her walk out the back and then signaled the man behind the bar for another whiskey. After brooding over several more drinks, he thought about Al, his old manager, and could still hear his lecture on the day they parted company:

"I can't do anything else for you Pete. You're out of the top tier and even the state fairs are in the past for you. You're down to county fairs and local events now and I don't deal at that level. We could have made money, you and me. I wanted to do what everybody does when they're winning. Endorsements! Tony Lama called me about you. They were interested in signing you, figured you could sell a lot of boots for them. I tried to find you. Remember? But where were you? On a three-day bender with a married woman. And then when I read in the papers about the husband finding you with her and him taking a couple of shots at you? Good God! Who would ever sign you after that? You're lucky he was a lousy shot!"

He had no excuses or explanations. He had not known the woman was married but to say so would only make it sound like an excuse. It had happened while he was on the West Coast Circuit just before he got hurt in the Cow Palace in San Francisco. The arena was at the end of a street named Geneva, the same name of the married woman. And there was a fog, a cold mist that left a thin sheen of moisture on the world. He had come to in the ambulance that took him to a place called Mission Emergency. He remembered a city-boy doctor who had never met a rodeo cowboy telling him that he had three cracked vertebrae and had to stay in the hospital until they could determine how serious the injuries were. He remembered how Joe Bean and Trey Mosley had snuck in a jug of Mexican brandy and how several nurses came by to see what the commotion was all about and how they ended up leaving with Joe and Trey at the end of their shifts. Geneva, the married woman, had visited him in the hospital but they found that the feelings had died and they had nothing to say to each other.

Al continued to lecture him: "We had some profitable years, Pete, but they're over. You never did take my advice to add other events to your bag of tricks. Hell, you are a natural born roper! But no, you had to stay with riding bulls. And now with the back, there is nothing else for you. You won't admit it but that back keeps getting you thrown when the animal twists to the right under you."

"Do you have my money?" Pete wasn't angry at Al. They had been friends too long for that.

"Yeah, here it is." Al handed him a bank check. "I didn't take my commission out of it. Couldn't bring myself to do it."

Pete nodded his head. He could not think of anything to say.

"Old man Tegmeyer asked about you. He is looking for a man who knows stock. Said he thought you might be about ready to quit the rodeo and start working for a living."

"He'd want me for grading stock?"

"Well, that's where you'd start. The Tegmeyer outfit is one of the big ones. You could work your way up, and with your experience you'd stand to make a good living with him."

"Is old Joe Bean still driving Tegmeyer's Cadillac for him?"

"Yeah, but the old man got him one of those fancy English Bentleys now. I told you he's doing well."

"Joe Bean was as fine a saddle bronc rider as ever was and now he's driving that old bastard around all day. No thanks! I won't work for a man that needs someone to drive him around all day."

"Yeah, I thought that's what you'd say. So what are you going to do? Go back to that raggedy-ass piece of land your daddy called a ranch? Hell, Pete, you know you can't make a go of that. No, you listen to me! One day the few good parts of your body are going to wear out and it'll finally dawn on you that the rodeo life is over. You'll find yourself drinking alone in some run-down bar in some no-name town and all the rubes will look at you, not remembering your name, but they will remember that you used to ride in the big rodeos and if you're lucky, they'll buy you a drink. Is that what you want? At least with Tegmeyer you'll still be respected for all the years on the circuit. Oh hell! I'm tired of trying to talk sense to you. Good luck Pete!" Al shook his hand.

His father left him the ranch in Tom Green County. A two-section spread that could barely support the family over the years and Pete had no interest in trying to make a go of it. He had always wanted a place with plenty of water and where grass actually came out of the ground. The ranch had a puny well that threatened to go dry every other year or so, but a businessman from back east, who had always dreamed of owning a ranch in Texas, had made an offer. Pete knew for a certainty that he would accept it. It wasn't a fortune but it would keep him going for a few years if he decided to drift around. Or he could put it back into another spread. He had seen some places in eastern Arizona. The winters would be a bit harder but there was plenty of grass and water. And nobody telling him how to run it. Well, it was something to think about. And then, there was always Tegmeyer. He picked up his whiskey.

At the end of the bar two couples were talking and laughing. The men looked like junior chamber of commerce types dressed in Western attire. The women were younger than the men; both were good looking and were openly giving Pete the eye. He heard the brunette say something about him being one of the old bull riders and then one of the men said something and they all laughed. The whiskey had been working on him and his fuse was already pretty well lit. He was not sure what the good-looking young people were laughing at. It didn't matter. It was all he needed. He got off his barstool and walked over to them. It did not take long for all the frustrations inside him to explode. The two neatly dressed young men were not fighters, just full of talk. He put one of them out of the fight with an uppercut and was working on the other when the police arrived.

The cop stood just inside the front door. He was a slightly built young man with black hair, dark eyes, and a big voice that instructed Pete to stop hitting the chamber of commerce type. The cop stood there, loose and confident with his thumbs hooked behind his belt buckle. He was wearing close fitting black leather gloves. Pete remembered telling the cop that he had better send for help because he was going to need it. And then he moved toward the officer. As Pete got close and cocked his right fist to throw a punch, he remembered a black blur on his left side, an explosion in his head and then, nothing.

As he regained consciousness, his nostrils were filled with the smell of old urine and men in need of a bath. He felt the cold concrete of the cell floor on his back. He looked up with his one good eye and saw a very large Indian looking down at him. The Indian was smiling and eating a candy bar.

"Looks like old Happy used the Golly Gloves," the Indian chuckled.

Pete reached up to feel his left cheek and realized that the whole side of his face was puffed up and that his eye was swollen shut. The hearing in his left ear was fuzzy. He had a headache that threatened to split his skull and his mouth was dry. The Indian had gone back to the corner of the cell where there was a concrete shelf against the wall and began talking with other occupants of the drunk tank. As he stared up at the ceiling with his right eye, a half-full bottle of soda pop appeared before him.

"Have a sip, amigo, it will help get you straight." The owner of the voice squatted down next to Pete and offered him the bottle. Pete lifted himself up, leaned against the wall and took a swig of the warm sweet soda. He felt a little better.

"Why is he happy about this?" Pete pointed to his face.

"No amigo. You misunderstand. What Mister Begay meant is that you had the unfortunate experience of meeting Officer Apodaca, who is known to his friends as Happy Apodaca. It is also apparent that either you did not follow Happy's instructions, or God forbid, you attacked him and he responded as he always does when this occurs. He struck with his well-known right cross. As for the golly interpretation, I think it best if Mister Begay explains. Mister Begay would you be so kind as to explain to our visitor?"

Mister Begay walked over to Pete's side, his bulk shutting off half the cell.

"He hit you one time with those gloves and gol–ly!" Mister Begay began giggling and there were squeals of laughter from the others in the cell. Pete did not think it was all that funny.

"Sap gloves, amigo," the owner of the soft drink explained, "Happy wears sap gloves when he thinks there will be trouble on his shift. They are leather gloves with powdered lead sewn into a pocket over the knuckles. They can be quite devastating, as you have learned." He handed the soda bottle back to Pete.

Pete took a long sip. It helped clear his head.

"Actually, Officer Apodaca does not need the Golly Gloves or additional assistance of any kind. I am proud to say that we have been friends since grade school and Happy enjoys a well-deserved reputation as a good man here in San Miguel County. In his youth he also enjoyed a successful career in the pugilistic world of the Golden Gloves. He traveled all over the country and even to Europe. We were and still are quite proud of him. Years in the ring take its toll on one's hands, and we all agree with his philosophy that there is no need to cause further damage to himself while keeping the peace."

"All right. That explains the Mexican cop." Pete was still angry about being put down so easily.

"My friend, I feel the need to explain something else to you since you obviously are not from these parts. You see, this is northern New Mexico, although my ancestors and most of the people hereabouts have always referred to it as New Spain. The majority of us here in northern New Mexico, can trace our families directly back to Spain. Nothing against Mexico, mind you, but to our way of thinking, Mexico was nothing but a brief stopping off place for our ancestors on their way up here to the north. It would serve you well in the future if you would keep that foremost in your mind while interacting with us."

Pete looked at the man while he tried to digest all he had said.

"My name is Pete." He held out his hand.

"Aurelio Sanchez Montoya at your service. But you can call me Doc."

"Doc, I didn't mean to insult the officer, it's just that I couldn't believe how quick he was."

"Forget it, Pete. None of us has sensed even the least bit of malevolence in you. And now I will give you the benefit of my brief examination of your injuries. All the signs point to the fact that you have suffered a concussion. I find no evidence of broken bones around the cheek bone or eye socket. You will have blurred vision in your left eye for a while and probably some hearing impairment in the left ear. I have asked the officers out front for some aspirin and a bottle of pop for you. They will take the cost of these items out of your cash when you leave here." Doc sat down, his back against the cell wall next to Pete.

"You a doctor?"

"No, no, not a doctor. But I have had medical training and have, in the past, dealt with physical trauma and all sorts of damage to the human body."

A uniformed police officer appeared on the other side of the cell bars.

"Here you go, Doc. Aspirin and a Double Cola."

"Thanks, Dave." Doc reached through the bars and took the items.

"How is he?" the officer pointed to Pete.

"So far, so good, but I would definitely call Doctor Callahan. He should certainly be examined by a pro."

The officer nodded and walked away.

"I suggest you take three of these with a good slug of pop and take a couple more every few hours or so. And don't move your head a lot."

"How do you know all this stuff?" Pete opened the tin of aspirin.

"Well, it all began while I was a pre-med student at the University of New Mexico. In my senior year I allowed my craving for sour mash to overcome my need to study, flunked out and was drafted by Uncle Sam. Because of my education, they made me a medic and then provided me with a unique opportunity to gain further experience in a place called Korea."

"So, why are you here?" Pete asked.

"My romance with sour mash, indeed, any kind of alcohol, has remained a big part of my life. Since, in the recent past, my funds have sunk to a new low, my latest love is Tokay, Thunderbird, Sweet Lucy, or whatever I can afford at the moment. I have from time to time been on the path to recov-

ery, as they call it. More than several times, in fact, but I keep
strolling off the path. My ex-wife told me that I was too busy
chasing Hell's Herd to stay sober, so she left me. Took the dog
and my old deer rifle and never looked back. It took me a
while to admit she was right. But after the last go around, I
have decided that it is time to head off this looming disaster
and get straightened out for good. I plan to use the GI Bill to
restart my interrupted education. I have these dreams of starting a clinic in the rural areas of the county. To make the people
here as proud of me as they are of my good friend, Officer
Apodaca. We all reach a point when we must take stock, run
the numbers, if you will, face reality, and make a decision.
Hell's Herd, indeed!" Doc chuckled.

They sat next to each other with their backs against the cell
wall, lost in their thoughts, trying to work on plans that did not
include spending any more time in the drunk tank.

After a few hours, they came for Pete and moved him into a
smaller, cleaner cell where a doctor examined him. This doctor
saw Pete twice a day and ordered a special menu for him that
was brought in from a restaurant near the downtown plaza. The
doctor told him that if he wanted to live a full life, he must give
up the rodeo circuit and take up a gentler way of making a living. The doctor gave him other advice about keeping his health
but Pete had heard it all before. After three days, the doctor
ordered his release and they took him back to the booking desk.
A sergeant gave him back all his belongings, including all his
cash. They did not take anything out for the aspirin and soda.
The sergeant told him that all charges against him had been
dropped by the district attorney and that he was free to go.

There was one condition, the sergeant insisted. It was that he leave town as soon as possible and, the sergeant explained in no uncertain terms, that meant today.

Pete stepped out into the bright sunlight of early morning and squinted his good eye half closed. He walked down Moreno Street in the direction of the saloon where his truck was parked. He regretted not having the chance to tell Doc goodbye.

When he finally found his pickup truck outside the saloon, he discovered that his spare tire and toolbox were gone. Serves me right, he thought. Should have locked them in the cab with my grip. He unlocked the cab and pulled back the rubber mat under the seat. He picked up a screwdriver and undid two screws that secured a small metal plate to the floorboard. He reached in and pulled out a handful of bills and counted them. Six hundred and seventy-five dollars. It was all there. He kept seventy-five dollars and put the rest back, screwed the plate down tight and replaced the rubber mat.

He sat behind the wheel and thought about his next move. He reached up and pulled the rearview mirror around and studied his face. The swelling had gone down but a dark bruise covered most of the left side of face, his vision was still blurred in his left eye, and a constant dull headache stayed with him. He remembered what Doc had talked about in the jail cell, about getting straight someday soon, and began to slowly accept the fact that there might not be any more rodeos. The day that Al had warned him about had finally come. He was sure of that.

His stomach growled, reminding him that the food they had fed him in jail was not enough to satisfy his appetite. He needed bacon and eggs and pancakes and plenty of coffee. Then he thought about the girl named Peggy and the café where she worked the morning shift and how pleasant it had been to talk with her. He sat behind the steering wheel, trying to figure out all the possibilities and all the while he fought the urge to buy a bottle at the package store next to the saloon.

He looked down at his blood-stained shirt and realized that he was wearing the same clothes he had on when he was booked into the jail. He smelled like the other inmates in the drunk tank and he needed a shave. He found a gas station several blocks away and while the attendant filled the pickup with gas, he went into the men's room, shaved with his old razor and cleaned up as best he could. He put on a clean pair of jeans and a shirt and put his old clothes in the trash can. The gas station jockey told him that he was a quart and a half low on oil. Pete told him to add a quart and asked directions to the Little Diner. He found the café on a side street just off the plaza. He parked on the far side of the square and began to walk to the café. When he was halfway across the plaza, he spotted Doc sitting on a wooden bench at the edge of a hacked out piece of lawn. He was holding tight to a bottle wrapped in a brown paper bag.

"Howdy, Doc!"

Doc looked up, confusion in his eyes.

"It's me." Pete pointed to his bruised face.

"Oh yes. It is you, indeed! How goes it, amigo?" Doc scooted over to the far end of the bench.

"I'm fine, Doc. I never got a chance to thank you, back there." Pete sat down.

"Your good health is my reward, amigo." Doc's words were slightly slurred. He took a long pull from the bottle.

"You OK, Doc?" Pete smelled the sweet perfume of fortified red wine.

"The sun is shining, the skies are blue, and I am home where no harm can come to me, so, yes, yes, I am fine."

"Doc. What you told me back there in jail, about straightening out, well it got me to thinking and I'm making some plans."

"Yes, my friend. Good for you. I am glad our talk was of some value to you."

Pete did not reply. He looked at Doc until Doc recognized the unspoken question.

"Well, as for me"—he waved the bottle around—"I am indeed straightened out. I have half of a bottle remaining and five dollars in my pocket. So yes, I will endeavor to remain on the straight and narrow path for as long as my faith and cash remain, for they are my fortune." Doc took a long drink from the bottle and then held it out to Pete.

"No thanks, Doc." An empty feeling replaced the joy he felt when he spotted Doc sitting on the bench. He felt that he should sit with Doc a while longer. Both were silent while Doc looked over to the edge of the square. He stared off into the distance with a very content look on his face. Pete realized that Doc was somewhere else and stood up to go. Doc did not notice him move. He sat smiling and holding the bottle with both hands. Pete reached into his pocket and pulled out a twenty-dollar bill.

"Doc, I feel that I need to square things with you for all your help." He held out the twenty to Doc.

"Such a kind gesture. Very generous, indeed, but there is absolutely no need." Doc grabbed the twenty and swiftly placed it in his shirt pocket. "I saw them, you know?" Doc pointed south.

"Who did you see, Doc?"

"Why, Hell's Herd, of course! Two years ago, I was stacking hay at my uncle's place over near Española when a storm rolled in from the east and covered the Sangre de Cristos. It was close to sunset and the mountains were a deep blood red with the storm clouds white and full and slowly turning dark above the range. That's when I saw them. They were in the clouds, heading north and going hell for leather. There were no cowboys with them, nobody trying to herd them in, they were just running wild."

Pete sat back down. He was very still, not wanting to disturb Doc and his telling of the story. He leaned back against the bench and watched Doc as he finished describing his vision. Doc continued to look south past the plaza. He was relaxed with a gentle smile on his lips. It was as if a haze of serenity had descended upon him, hiding the demons that remained from the herd. He was calm and there was a peace and a sense of well-being about him that comes only when you finally realize that the worst is over and things will never be as bad again. It was a peace found only in submission. After a while Pete stood up very slowly and almost whispered:

"Well, see you around, Doc."

"Until the next time my friend. Con Dios!" Doc gave him a tiny smile.

The heat started to build in the square and there were several maintenance workers out among the trees and sparse shrubbery. Pete walked to the end of the square toward the café. He hoped Peggy was still working her shift.

Peggy was in the kitchen filling out her time sheet. The owner had agreed to let her leave a few hours early so she could arrange for an early start for Santa Fe in the morning. She was talking to the cook when she saw Pete through the front window of the diner. He was standing across the street at the corner of the plaza. She had heard about the fight at the Pronghorn and could see the damage done to Pete's face. She had thought about him during the past two days. She did not know why because she realized that a relationship was the last thing she needed at this point. She had received a letter from the School for the Deaf and they had requested she bring her son to Santa Fe so they could both be interviewed by school staff. She knew that this was as good as a letter of admittance. She would have to move to Santa Fe, find a job, a place to live, and everything else that went with this new opportunity for her son. Why in hell, in the middle of all this, she asked herself, did she need to get to know a broken-down saloon brawler of a rodeo cowboy. But she looked at him standing on the corner and hoped that he would come into the café. She was pouring out a cup of coffee to a customer at the counter and watched Pete walk across the street to the front door of the diner.

As the door closed behind him, he took off his hat, spotted Peggy behind the counter, and smiled at her.

Oh Lord, she thought, please help me now because I know that I damn sure cannot help myself. "Howdy, Pete, where have you been?" She saw the immediate chagrin in his eyes.

"It's kind of a long story."

"Well, Pete, the lunch crowd won't be here for a little while, so I have plenty of time."

CUT-NOSE WOMAN

he cut-nose woman stood in the shadows of the Agency store and watched the young policeman on the far side of the street. She had spent a restless night and slept little because of the night sweats, but the cool of the early morning shade eased her discomfort. It did not ease her hatred for the young policeman. She hated him because he had taken her man to jail for beating her and cutting her nose. She hated the policeman for wearing the white man's clothes and following the white man's ways. But she mostly hated him because he did not respect the old ways of their people. The white man's law now kept her man locked away in a small room with a barred door and windows, which was the cruelest thing anyone could do to a man who was once a great warrior. And this young policeman, an heir to the free and wandering ways of his people, chose instead to turn his back on them. They were a people feared by their enemies and they had always moved freely from these mountains to the Sierras in the south. Her husband bore the scars of battles with the Mexicans and the white soldiers, and in his old age should be living out his years enjoying the respect of his people and not be locked away in the white man's jail. But this policeman had taken him away because he had beaten her and cut her nose when he caught her with her old lover. This had always been their way, but this young policeman and others who followed the law of the white man considered it a crime. How could that be, she thought? Her man would have no respect if it was known that his woman slept with another man without being punished. And the cut nose also gained secret respect from some of the women of her clan who would never have the courage to flaunt the rules as she did. And now this policeman, a traitor to the old ways, would take this all away and replace it with the white man's law. So she stood in the shade next to the Agency store, holding a small cloth bundle with venison jerky and piñon nuts for her man as she waited for visiting hours and watched as the policeman mounted his horse and led the pack animal out the back gate of the stable yard.

Antonio had seen the cut-nose woman as he saddled the mare. He watched her carefully as he went about securing a pack to the frame on the mule. The woman and her man made trouble for him on a regular basis. Both drank heavily and fought constantly and were regular occupants of the small cell in the tribal building. The man bragged about being one of the old warriors, but Antonio's Uncle Chapo, who in fact was one of the old warriors, told him that the man was dismissed from the scouts due to his drinking and laziness. Antonio knew that the young people did not want to be bothered with the old stories of battle, and as his uncle's generation slowly passed, it no longer mattered what the old warriors thought. But this woman and her man spoke loudly about the old ways and caused Antonio problems with their own kind of battles, so he kept his eye on the woman as he rode down the main street and turned east toward the mountains.

The cut-nose woman watched him as he rode out of the stable, and when he passed in front of the Agency store, she stepped out of the shadows and spat into the dust of the street behind him.

THE BEST
GOOD HORSE

It was the hour just before light when John Westley Thornhill decided to leave the ranch. He had studied on it for a considerable time, had finally made up his mind, and now there was no going back. This hour had always been the best part of his day. It was the hour for planning the day's work while the peace of sleep had not quite gone. In the spring this hour was the time of stillness before the wind began. The wind that would blow all day and into the evening, battering everything in its path. And in the summer it was the cool time before the sun's heat rose and sucked the moisture out of every living creature south of the mountains. But on this day, his last on the ranch, he watched a quiet snow cover the ground between the barn and the corrals. It came down in a blur of white in the silence of his morning.

He swung his legs off the bed onto the cracked linoleum of the cabin floor. Everyone called it a cabin but it had been built as an equipment shed more than fifty years ago. Later, when the barn was completed, a large tack room was added to the new structure and the cabin was left empty so that when John Westley arrived as top hand, he homesteaded the abandoned shack, living apart from the other hands who shared the bunkhouse across the large, open lot from the main house where the owners of the ranch lived. John Westley had kept his feelings to himself but he had never liked nor respected the owner of the ranch, a man named Garth. Garth was a bitter old man who lived every day with a belligerent attitude, which made it a certainty that good help did not stay long on the place. Until John Westley's arrival, the only people Garth did not treat with contempt were old Porfirio and his family and that was probably because Garth's wife, Ellen, would never allow it. Ellen loved Graciela and Porfirio Romero, and their youngest, Lucía, was the apple of her eye. Ellen was the complete opposite of her husband.

She was as kind and considerate as she was beautiful. But there was something about her that John Westley sensed on the day he was hired, and that was that her good looks and genteel manner hid an iron will. After he had been on the place for a while, he was proven right as he watched her handle problems when they arose on the ranch. It was good that she was strong because her cantankerous husband came down with pneumonia, stubbornly refused to seek medical help, and died right there in the main ranch house. After that Miss Ellie, as Ellen was called, took over and everything from finances to morale improved.

With the snow coming down outside, John Westley stepped into his jeans and pulled on his boots, then walked over to a wooden shelf that stuck out like an afterthought from the back wall. He grabbed a fistful of ground coffee from the can, threw it into the old pot, added water, and then lit one of the two gas burners on an old cast iron stand. The two-burner plate was the only thing close to a modern appliance in the shack. Ten years ago, the Rural Electric Co-Op had run a powerline all the way out to the ranch, but he preferred to use coal oil lamps for light. The two-burner served to make his coffee as well as provide heat when the small woodstove near the front door was overwhelmed by the raw winds of winter that seeped through the cracks in the walls of the cabin. He had rigged a gravity flow water line that ran from the water tank which was up the hill to a spigot on the back wall. He needed nothing more to make a comfortable home for himself.

While the coffee was brewing, he walked over to an old wooden ammunition crate, lifted the lid, and removed a tin breadbox. He levered off the lid and placed it on the cot, then removed several large manila envelopes, some writing paper, and several old pencils. He put these on the cot next to the bread box and reached back into the ammo crate and removed three stacks of fifty-dollar bills, each wrapped with a rubber band. The cash totaled three thousand, two hundred and fifty dollars. There were also ten silver dollars scattered around the bottom of the box. He laid everything out in a neat pile on the cot. Except for a prize saddle and a beat-up '37 Chevy pickup truck, which was parked behind the barn with the keys in the ignition, it was everything he owned.

The dawn was beginning to stream through the one window of the shack and throw muddy light onto a wooden frame he had built. On this frame rested a fancy prize saddle that he had won in a poker game at the VFW hall in Alamogordo many years ago. It was too fancy for work so it had never been near a horse, but had always been here in the shack where he had admired it as an art lover would admire the paintings of the masters in an art gallery. The intricate leather carvings and inlaid silver could hold his attention for hours. The saddle was made by S.D. Myers Saddlery in El Paso and he was told that it was worth a lot of money. The previous owner had put it up against John Westley's two hundred dollars and an inside straight. He never cared to know the saddle's worth since he had little regard for its value or for that matter, possessions of any sort. To him, it was worth more than anyone would pay for it because as he sat alone, admiring it, he imagined it one day on his best good horse and thought about how much pleasure it would bring as he slowly worked the stiff leather into a comfortable workplace. Of course, he never got around to doing that and now that sitting any horse only caused his knees to threaten to explode on him, the saddle would remain on the frame. And he would continue to be confined to overseeing the day-to-day operations of the ranch from his pickup truck. The old doctor in Alamo had told him that both his knees were "bone on bone," which meant nothing to him until it was explained that he could only look forward to less mobility and more pain from arthritis in the future. He did not accept the news well but had gradually adapted to trading his best good horse for his pickup truck, even though it meant limiting himself to roads, old cow paths, or smooth ground.

The warm aroma of boiling coffee grounds reached him and he poured out a cup of the thick brew. He went over, sat on the bed, and looked down at the sum of everything he owned and planned out the distribution of these possessions. He had no family or friends that he gave a damn for. The relationship between him and his brother and sister, distant as it was, ended after his sentencing in the Lubbock County Courthouse. Any hope of staying in touch died a sure death while he served out his time down in Sugar Land.

The snow began to collect on the window frame and it was a while before his memories left him. The coffee was cold and he cussed himself for sitting still so long, lost in the past. He went over to the window and saw that the snow was heavy and thick and would cover over the rocks on the edge of the big lot between the cabin and the barn. Good, he thought, the more moisture the better. He hoped it was falling on the flats down below, where the driest sections were. With enough moisture, he thought, more stock could be moved to the lower pasture. The everyday plans to keep the outfit running smooth came as naturally to him as breathing, even though he knew the time for these things was over. It was Sunday, a slow day at the ranch and a good day to leave.

He had never in his life gone, of his own free will, to a doctor. The only medicos he had ever dealt with usually worked for the county and had sewed him up and tended to his other injuries in a county clinic while he was handcuffed to a cot with one or more uniformed officers of the law standing by. But there had been another sawbones, one who had made an impression. He was an eye doctor in El Paso.

"I will write a prescription for eyeglasses," he had told him. "They will help for a time, but it is inevitable that your vision will continue to deteriorate."

"How much will it deteriorate?" he remembered asking.

The doctor hesitated. "You will eventually lose your vision entirely."

"All of it?"

"Yes."

"How long will that take?"

"Hard to say," the doctor had replied.

"Why is it so damned hard to say? Don't you know?"

"Because, Mr. Thornhill, I am a doctor, not a fortune teller." The irritation was plain on the doctor's face. "Tell me. Are you a gambling man?"

"I have placed a bet or two in my time."

"OK, Mr. Thornhill, I will make you a wager that within six months your vision will be reduced to arm's length, you will begin to lose your peripheral vision and shortly thereafter it will be gone completely."

He had been silent, hearing the echo of the doctor's words. Finally, he stood up and stuck out his hand.

"Thanks, Doc. I appreciate you being honest."

He had walked out of the office to the nurse's desk and asked for the bill. As he was counting out his cash, another nurse came through the door and handed him a small slip of paper.

"The prescription for bifocals," she said.

"Thanks." He carefully folded it in half and put the slip of paper in his shirt pocket, picked up his receipt and left the office. In the lobby of the building, he crumpled up the prescription and dropped it in a trash can near the front door.

And the doctor had been right, his vision was fading at a steady rate. That meeting had taken place just before the previous Thanksgiving and it was then that he had started to think about leaving. He was a naturally stubborn man and changing course never came easy to him. But he had experienced the change that the doctors had predicted. He had always thought that he was a practical man, but it had taken some time to accept the reality of the calendar that ruled his life. It's time, he thought, to pick up your cash and step away from the table. You ain't winnin' and it's damn sure not likely you'll break even.

He ran some water into a tin washbasin, put it on the two-ring stove to heat up, and got his shaving gear off the shelf.

He was thinking about the prize saddle and how old Porfirio had always admired it, so he decided to give it to him. He had considered Lucía for the saddle but decided to give her the cash instead. So that's it, he thought, the cash to Lucía and the saddle to her father.

He dipped his shaving brush in the heated water of the wash pan and worked up a lather in the old mug. He did not remember when he began thinking so much about the past. Maybe it was when the doctor in Alamo told him about his knees. It could have been then or was it what you did when the years piled up? He couldn't say for certain, he only knew that memories came to him more frequently now, as if they were stories about someone he knew long ago. He thought about the old mare Strawberry and how she was the best good horse of all the best good horses he ever rode. Mile 'r More came close but could not match Strawberry. Even though the gelding worked every bit as hard, he did not have all the skills or instincts of the mare.

He also often thought of Lucía, the daughter and youngest child of Porfirio and Graciela Moreno, both of whom had been at the ranch long before he got there. Porfirio was one of the best horse and cow men John Westley had ever worked with. And with Graciela, the ranch owners got a good cook who arranged for all the feeding of the ranch hands and was also capable of handling other chores that came up on a regular basis on the ranch. Lucía had four older brothers who were a little rough around the edges but had all turned out to be good hands; their father would settle for nothing less. As they grew up and left home they all found work and sent money home to their folks. Lucía had no rough edges. She had the grace and manners of her mother. She was reserved but had the self-confidence of any child who grew up with four rowdy brothers.

John Westley reckoned that he had been at the ranch for about five years when Lucía was born. Graciela would take her along on every chore she performed on the ranch and the child could melt the heart of even the roughest and crudest ranch hand. She had grown up with a reserve that was not due to any shyness on her part but rather her parents' expectation that the boundary line between men and women should be observed and respected. So he was surprised when one Saturday morning he observed Lucía, all of six years of age, making her way carefully past the barn and up the rocky path that led to his shack.

She was carefully holding a small plate covered with a dish towel, her bare feet kicking up a tiny cloud of dust.

He had stood and watched her approach. He had expected to see one of her family keeping an eye on her. He could see no one. She was alone. She stopped in front of him and held the plate up in front of her, her arms held out at full length and said nothing.

"Good morning, Lucía."

"Good morning, Señor Juan."

"What is this?" he pointed to the plate, even though he could tell by the fresh baked smell that it was from her mother's kitchen.

"Do you want some empanadas?" Her voice was small but firm.

"Well, yes I do. Thank you." He took the plate. "Did your mother send them?"

"No. I took them from the table to bring you. I heard mama say that you had no one to cook for you."

"So, you felt sorry for me?"

"No." Her dark brown eyes looked at him with all the honesty of a six-year-old. "I just wanted to give them to you."

He put the pastries inside the shack and they walked back to her house with the empty plate and dishtowel. He had explained to her that they should tell her mother that she had taken the empanadas for him. From that day on, every Saturday, she brought him a few empanadas, and that had been the beginning of their friendship.

A year into their friendship he had told her that she could stop calling him "Señor Juan."

"What should I call you?" she had asked. She was perplexed. Her parents would be scandalized if she called him by his given name.

"Oh, I don't know." He cussed himself for not thinking this thing out.

"I know," she said, "I'll call you Tio!"

"OK! That'll work."

It suited him fine and he was glad that she had made the decision. The title of Uncle fit and at the same time it kept a bit of formality between them. He was glad for the formality because Lucía grew into a very beautiful young woman who attracted a lot of attention from every dreaming and lustful ranch hand. None of them ever tried to act out their dreams because Porfirio was known to be a rough old cob and it was rumored he had killed a few men down in Mexico in the old days. And John Westley let a few young rowdies go when he heard them making some remarks about Lucía's beauty. It did not take long for the word to get around and any cowboy valuing a payday over a wrong comment stayed well clear of her.

She was grown now and away at the college in Las Cruces. He was sure that Miss Ellie played a big part in financing her education. Now that she was out in the world, she shared her thoughts with him on a more mature level. She talked about her studies and about the river that ran through the valley and how the water fed the pecan trees that made up huge forests in the desert and of the green fields of cotton and the many restaurants in town, and he knew that she would never come back to a life on the ranch. She told him about a boy she met whose parents owned a ranch up near Clayton and he felt the bite of jealousy when he saw her eyes brighten and her cheeks flush as she mentioned the boy's name. His name was Justin. Well, he had thought, I damn sure know what's on Justin's mind but I can't go around threatening to beat the snot out of every young man with a lustful thought about Lucía. No, he thought, it's best that she learn, on her own, about what goes on between people who think they are in love. I have taught her all I can about ranch work, the rest of it is none of my business.

He only saw her now in the summers and on holidays. In the summers, she still helped out on the ranch doing everything from cleaning out the barn to gathering and branding cattle. She was smart and worked hard. She was interested in everything about life and asked him questions that, at times, he could not answer.

Lucía had always admired John Westley's best good horse, Strawberry, a roan mare that was renowned for her abilities. After Lucía had gained enough skill in doing ranch work horseback, he let her ride Strawberry one time when they were out gathering cattle. It filled his heart with pride to see her and the mare work as one. Lucía was gentle but firm in handling the mare and old Strawberry responded with even more effort than John Westley could get out of her.

Then one day, while Lucía was away at college, Strawberry had broken her right front leg while they were crossing an arroyo down in the flat. John Westley had put her down with the old Colt Single Action Army he always carried when horseback. He broke the news to Lucía when she came home for Easter. He remembered tears coming to her eyes and she was quiet for a long time. Later that afternoon she had asked him if he had picked out another best good horse. No, he had told her, he had not yet picked one.

"Can I pick one?" she asked.

"Well, I'd have to think on it."

"I know all the good horses. Worked with most of them," she told him.

"Yeah. I know. Well . . . all right. You can pick one."

"Promise?" Her voice was filled with excitement. "Promise?" she repeated.

"No. I don't promise." He was firm.

"But you said . . ."

"I know what I said. I said that you can pick my new best good horse."

"But . . . ?"

"Lucía, I have never made a promise in my life. And there's no need to make one now."

"Why don't you make promises?"

He sighed and shook his head. He did not like to explain himself to anyone.

"Never saw the need for them. If you tell someone you are going to do something, then you do it. No need to promise. Your word should be as good as a promise."

She was quiet for a while, looking over at the horses in the corral. Then she broke out in one of her beautiful smiles.

"Sin promesas! It will be as you said. Sin promesas!"

"Yes. Sin promesas." He was happy with that. It said it all.

It was during the Thanksgiving break that he had noticed the change in her. She had come home on Thanksgiving Day and not the weekend before as she usually did. She had taken his new best good horse, a sorrel top he called Mile 'r More, out to check a fence the next morning. He was in the barn when he heard hoofbeats at a gallop and looked up to see Lucía on Mile 'r More. She had him in a full gallop heading straight for the barn. As she came into the space in front of the barn door, he saw her pulling hard on the reins to get the horse to stop. He dropped the shovel he was holding and in a few steps was standing next to the horse's neck grabbing the reins near the bit. She knew that he was angry but she remained defiant, sitting straight in the saddle.

"Get down off this horse!" he commanded.

She dismounted and he could see that she was flustered to the point of tears. He had recognized a touch of anger in her and some type of resentment on Thanksgiving Day but had kept it to himself.

There was a change going on and he was willing to give her plenty of room to deal with it, but nobody had any cause to mistreat one of the animals. He led the sorrel into the barn and began unsaddling him. She followed him in and without turning to face her he began speaking to her in a calm voice.

"I don't know what is going on in your life, Lucía, and it's none of my business, but I'll not have you treating an animal like you just did. This horse's only purpose in life is to turn in an honest day's work, day after day. He don't know no better but that doesn't give anyone the right to treat him like you just did. It's a damn good thing that you got a high port bit on him or you woulda' cut his tongue up and ruined him. And you just better hope that his jaw ain't hurt!"

"I am sorry." And then she broke into tears.

He finished the unsaddling and took the tack to the rear of the building, and when he came back to the front she was sitting on an old cut-off tree stump outside the front stall. He could not see her clearly, but he could tell by her quiet sobs that tears were running freely down her face. He never knew what to do when a woman cried. It was the one thing that froze him up and always left him without words, so he just stood there quietly, letting her cry. After a while, she stopped and it was quiet except for the snorting of the sorrel out back.

"Have you ever been in love?" she asked.

"In love?" The question took him by surprise and he was stalling for time.

"Yes! Have you?"

"Well, I—no—I mean—" He closed his mouth. He knew in an instant he was up against a wall. Lucía looked at him, her hands twisted into a knot, tears still running as she waited for his reply. He felt her desperation as much as his own and tried to regain control.

"Well, Lucía, there were times I thought I was . . . but I was never sure." He wondered how such mealy-mouthed words could come from his own mouth.

"How do you mean you were not sure?"

Oh God, he thought, there is something happening to her that I know nothing about except I need to be very gentle.

"I'm not sure how to say this right but there were times when my heart tried to convince me of things that didn't make sense at the time. I mean it was like I wasn't holding a tight rein and was liable to end up in a mesquite thicket or off the side of a cliff." He looked at her and she still had the question in her eyes. "I just wish I could answer you better but nobody ever asked me that question. Hell, I never even asked myself."

"So, you never loved anyone so much that when they left you felt like your heart would break?"

"No, Lucía. I was sad a couple of times when things didn't work out with a woman I cared for, but no, I was never heart broke."

"Do you remember that boy Justin I told you about? The one from up north?"

"Yeah." Things were becoming much clearer to him.

"We were to meet for breakfast before class one day and he didn't show. I waited for him until just before class began. Later, a friend told me that he had left. That he dropped out of school and went back home. Took his pickup, his trailer, and roping pony and just left. He never even said goodbye! I thought of how foolish I looked, waiting for him outside the café. Why would he do that?" The tears began again.

"Because he's just a dumb little son of a —, I mean who knows why, but I'll tell you this for sure. He made a serious mistake, leaving you like that, but you are much better off being shed of him or anyone like him. You deserve better and don't ever think different!" So much for being gentle, he thought. "And maybe you just need to get a better grip on that heart of yours and don't be letting it put you in touch with idiots like this mama's boy Justin. I mean, I'm sorry if you still love him and all that but you need to be thinking clear about this!"

Lucía had stopped crying and was looking at him with surprise and he thought he spotted a tiny bit of relief in her eyes. "Now, it's gettin' late. I need you to brush down this sorrel and put him up. There's a couple of apples drying on that window ledge there. You might want to give one to Mile 'r More and maybe he might just let you try to make up to him. And from now on don't ever take out your hard feelings on a dumb animal just because you made a bad decision. That's all I got to say about it!"

She stood there for a long minute, staring at the ground, and then went into the barn and saw to the sorrel.

In the morning they said their goodbyes and he watched as she drove down to the flats on her way to the highway and her long drive back to school. She had come back again over the Christmas break and it seemed to him that she was more settled. Nothing was said about Justin. She was civil to everyone and she had ridden out with old Porfirio to bring in a few strays. He felt better about everything when she went back to college after New Year.

And now he sat on his cot with the note paper in front of him. He thought long and hard about what he had to say to her and finally decided that everything that needed saying had already been said so he just wrote: "Porfirio gets the saddle. Lucía gets the rest." He signed his name and put the money and the note into one of the large manila envelopes. He picked up one of the silver dollars and put it in his watch pocket, then sealed the envelope. He took up the pencil again and wrote on the envelope: "For Lucía, sin promesas."

There was a spot on the eastern border of the ranch, high up, next to the government land in the mountains and it was John Westley's favorite place. It was a high round knob of granite and it was said that the Apaches scraped and hacked out their arrowheads here while they were watching out. It was a good place to watch out because from the top of the knob you could see out over the far west corner of Texas and into Old Mexico. The site had been pretty well picked over but there were still a few old arrowheads scattered around. John Westley would go up there every Sunday that he had free time. It was a two-hour walk from his shack on a good day. The country was too rough for a horse so it was easier just to fill a canteen and walk up.

From the knob you could look down into Rock Snake Canyon, a ragged gash in the brown earth of the northern Chihuahua desert. And if you were there after a big rain in the mountains, you could watch the runoff come roaring down the canyon, the sound like an eighteen-wheeler crashing down the narrow walls, all churning brown with foam at the top, the water rising halfway up the sheer cliff walls. And when the water receded, the boulders at the bottom would be uncovered and clean and white in the sun. And the rock rattlers and lizards that had not been washed down to the flats below would crawl back out onto the boulders and warm their blood in the new quiet. They called this place Round Mountain and before his eyesight had gone all to hell, he could make out the sharp lines and the smaller boulders and look into the dark shadows of the cliff face. It would be good to visit the spot one last time.

He stood up and placed the envelope in the middle of his cot and reached into the old ammo box, took out an old Texas jockstrap holster, slipped his belt through the loop on the back, and cinched it down tight. The last thing in the ammo crate was his old Colt revolver. He took it out and ran his hand down the barrel, feeling the front sight. The man he bought it from had claimed the Colt shot off to one side and had bent the blade of the front sight to compensate for bullet strike. Well, he thought, nothing to worry about here since accuracy was of no concern. He slipped the Colt into the holster and pushed it down until it was good and snug.

He looked around the shack, saw that everything was to his liking, stepped through the front door, and pulled it tight behind him. As he stepped out into the snow, he saw Miss Ellie making her way over to the Moreno's house. She was carrying a bowl covered with a red cloth and he felt that old flash of desire that he had kept so close and then he felt the regret that always followed. It was not the regret of something lost but rather the regret of a chance not taken. The regret had softened over the years but it was still there. He cursed his weak eyes, as Miss Ellie was just a blurred outline in the snow, but he saw her bright red hair flame defiantly through the white shadows. He smiled and waved to her and then turned to his right onto the path that led up to Round Mountain.

Miss Ellie waved back and stood watching as he slowly made his way through the snow on the far side of the shack. She wondered where he would be going at this time on a Sunday and in all this snow. There was no need for him to be out in this storm. They had put out fresh bales of hay into the pastures two days ago, so the cattle didn't need tending. She watched his slow stiff movements and could tell that his arthritis was acting up again. Well, she thought, old John Westley was probably just restless, as usual. She stood watching him until the snow, coming down in curtains of white, blocked him from her sight and in a little while the snow completely covered his tracks.

THE FOUNDLING HOME

The sharp noises of the night patrols echoed through the city streets and often woke the boys in the foundling home. The measured cadence of brogans on the cobblestones and the harsh Yankee voices drifted on the Mississippi River fog through the brick walls of the home. It had been like this ever since the blue-clad army had come up the river in their gunboats and taken the city without a fight.

But on this night, a young boy named Owen woke to another sound in the home. Muffled sobbing and harsh whispers came from the other end of the room. He had learned to come awake slowly when there were night noises in the room. Most of the time it was just the smaller boys lost in their nightmares, but sometimes it was the older bully boys doing bad things to the little ones in the dark. He lay still and listened, opening his eyes to small slits. Then he slowly turned over to look past the iron stove in the center of the room, and he could make out bulky shadows leaning over a bunk near the door that led to the dining hall. An older boy cursed quietly; above this oath, Owen heard a thin, high-pitched noise come from Ansel's bunk. Slowly, the keening softened to a sound like a small kitten mewing for food. Ansel and he were not close friends, but they were the same age, and Owen stared at the far end of the room, thinking of what he could do to stop the bully boys. Some of the older boys were still in their beds, where they raised up, looked over at the commotion, and then lay back, pulling the covers over their heads.

Owen slipped out of his bunk and walked quickly over the cold stone floor to Ansel's bunk.

"Hey!" he yelled as loud as he could. His challenge echoed off the brick walls in a young boy's squeak.

A tall, raw-boned blonde named Jack turned and looked at him.

"Go back to bed!"

"Leave Ansel alone!" Owen held his fists up in front of himself.

Jack looked down at him and laughed. Then quick as a snake, he backhanded the small boy and sent him sprawling into the foot of a bunk on the other side of the center aisle. Owen was stunned but he felt no pain. He got to his feet, jumped up on Jack's back, and began pulling his hair and biting his ears. Jack shook him off and Owen slid across the floor, scraping skin off his right cheek. As he slowly pulled himself up, Owen saw that Jack had moved across the aisle to finish him. He rushed at Jack, his arms pumping furiously, but the taller boy reached down, picked him up and held him in a bear hug. Owen could feel Jack's grip begin to cut off his breathing. Owen put his hands together, locking his fingers the way the Brothers made the boys hold their hands at prayer and brought this small double fist down on the bridge of Jack's nose. He heard Jack grunt, so he hit him again and panicked when he felt his own breath leaving him as Jack squeezed tighter. His third desperate blow made a crunching sound and he felt something give way under his fists. Jack's grip loosened and the small boy fell to the ground as Jack cried out and brought both hands to his broken nose.

Blood squeezed through the larger boy's fingers and Owen quickly began looking for some other place on Jack's body to mount an attack. He put his hands together in a double fist again and hit Jack between the legs with every bit of strength he had. Jack screamed and doubled over, holding his groin. He stumbled over the foot of Ansel's bed and landed on his side in the center aisle of the room. Owen rushed over and attacked Jack's unprotected face with both fists, landing hard blows to the rapidly swelling bridge of Jack's nose.

By now all the boys in the room were awake and were watching the small boy's arms flailing like a threshing machine. Then one of the older boys got out of his bunk and grabbed the small attacker.

He spoke softly to Owen. "That's enough! Let's not wake the Brothers!" He led the smaller boy back to his bunk while the others picked Jack up off the floor.

Owen lay still in his bunk, his eyes wide, his breath coming fast in the dim light, not knowing what would happen next; when he realized nothing would, he relaxed and then felt satisfaction when he heard Jack sobbing softly in the same way Jack had made the smaller boys sob. He lay in his bunk and felt the dull ache of his hands and sting on his cheek, but inside, he felt good. It was a clean, honest feeling. He thought that it might be the feeling the Brothers told the boys they were supposed to have after receiving Holy Communion. But although he had received the Holy Sacrament regularly since his First Communion, he had never felt this good.

The next morning the Brothers gathered all the boys in the dining hall. The boys stood at attention in a straight row, lined up according to age, youngest boy on one end, oldest on the other. Brother Xavier stood in front of the older boys, and two of his assistants stood at each end of the row. The Brothers appeared stiff in their white collars and black frocks and they all looked as if they had just caught the boys in an act of mortal sin.

"Well, then! Who will tell me what happened?' Brother Xavier addressed the older boys.

The boys stared straight ahead in their silence. Brother Xavier then walked over to Jack.

"Let me be more specific. Who did this damage to Master Dupree's face?" He glared at Jack.

The silence was complete. Not even the fearful breathing of the boys could be heard. Brother Xavier was a large man with badly scarred face and only one eye.

"Every one of you know that it is a mortal sin to tell a lie. It is also a sin to not speak the truth when it is known." Brother Xavier walked back and forth in front of the older boys. "So, even if you do not lie to me but you hide the truth, you will just as surely be damned to hell the same as if you lied." His voice was much louder. "Now, who did this!?"

The older boys cringed at Brother Xavier's rage but they remained silent. The small boy with the sore hands was giving some thought to the Brother's words and had to agree with him on the point about mortal sin. It made sense to him that hiding the truth was the same as a lie, and if it was the same kind of sin, then it seemed only fair that you should receive the same kind of punishment. He struggled with this thought, trying to imagine what eternal damnation would be like. An image of large blistering fires and devil tormenting the suffering souls of hell formed bright and clear in his mind, and although he could not quite grasp the concept of eternity, he knew it was a very long time. He thought about it a while longer, and when there was no doubt left in him, he said, "I did it, Brother Xavier!" He felt confident that any punishment the Brothers handed out would be easier to suffer than eternal damnation and the fires of hell.

"What?" Brother Xavier appeared startled and walked down to the other end of the line.

"I said I did, Bother Xavier, but I ain't sorry!"

Brother Xavier reached out and squeezed the boy's left ear. "Ain't, Master Jones?"

"I meant to say that I am not sorry I did it." The older boys looked at Jack and giggled.

"Silence!" Brother Xavier leaned down and came face-to-face with the small boy. The scars that ran across the Brother's red face looked blue in the cold light of the dining room. Owen tried not to look at the hole where the missing eye had once been. "You caused this devastation to Master Dupree's face?"

"Yes, Brother Xavier."

"He did not!" Jack yelled out.

All the boys laughed.

"Well now!" Brother Xavier grinned and Owen looked away as the empty socket of the missing eye squeezed shut. "I wonder who is telling the truth and who is tempting the fires of hell?" He reached down and gently took the small boy's hands in his, inspecting them closely as he turned them over and then looked at the fresh abrasions on his cheek. He nodded to the other brothers, and they went down the line, carefully examining the hands of each boy. When they finished, they stepped back; each shook his head in Brother Xavier's direction.

"Now then, Master Dupree. You have a chance to reconsider, because unless St. Michael himself entered the dormitory last night, the only scars of battle are on you and"—he turned and looked at the small boy—"this young warrior. Would you care to tell me who did it?"

Giggling and laughter broke out among all the boys.

"Silence! Or there will be no breakfast!" Brother Xavier roared.

Jack's eyes turned away from the Brother and his face turned bright red.

"I am waiting, Master Dupree! No details, I want a simple yes or no. Is this young man telling the truth?"

"Yes, but—"

"That will be all." Brother Xavier said softly. He turned and walked slowly down the line of boys. The small boy noticed that the Brother was still smiling. Without breaking his stride, looking straight ahead, the Brother said: "Stations of the Cross instead of supper tonight. You are dismissed!"

Later, after breakfast, Owen went over to talk to Ansel, but Ansel refused to even look at him. During the next few weeks, Ansel withdrew more and more into himself, and every day, the fear grew in his eyes. Ansel had a look that reminded Owen of the paintings he had seen of the Christians in front of the lions in the Roman coliseum. He thought that it must be even worse than eternal damnation to carry around that much fear. Then one day, without any notice or announcement, Ansel was gone from the home. None of the boys knew where he had gone, but Owen hoped that it was to a place where he would not be afraid.

THE PINEY WOODS, TEXAS: DECEMBER 24, 1941

The mist encircled the trees of the Piney Woods and only began to give way when the sun began its climb. The hollows and draws of the lowland held tightly to the damp and they stayed thick white, like troughs of snow in the woods. A black Ford sedan sped along the asphalt of the narrow roads that cut a path through the woods. The driver did not slow down for the clouds of mist in the hollows. He downshifted to second gear and pushed on the accelerator pedal when he saw a slight rise on the far side of the mist and kept the speed of the Ford steady. He whistled softly to himself. His eyes were as flat as the Ford's windshield and there was no warmth in them. They were light gray and nothing escaped them. Through these eyes, the driver had always seen the world as his hunting ground, ever alert for danger or for the chance of prey. Several years ago, after a job in Chicago, a newspaper man had called them "killer's eyes." When he was born, his grandfather gave him the name Smoke Eyes. The nickname had stuck, but over the years it was shortened to Smoke. He never liked the nickname. He preferred the name his mother had given him, Daniel.

The man who sat in the passenger's seat was younger than the driver. He was loading a Winchester pump twelve-gauge shotgun. The chambered round was a rifled slug, the others were double-ought buckshot. On the seat between them was a Thompson submachine gun and three twenty-round magazines. Neither of them cared for the fifty-round drum magazine. They considered it something only an amateur would use. The men were both dressed in charcoal gray suits of worsted wool with vests of the same material. The driver's suit was custom fitted and French cuffs showed off small pearl cufflinks. A gold chain ran from one vest pocket to another where it was attached to an engraved gold pocket watch. He wore his fedora at a slight tilt, a style favored by certain movie stars and a few well-dressed gangsters. His tuneless whistling did not bother his partner, who often told him that it reminded him of air escaping from a tire. They had worked together for just over three years. Between them they had killed five men since January.

As the sun rose in the sky, the fog lifted and the trees of the Piney Woods began to take shape on both sides of the road. The driver opened the wing window and the breeze cooled them. They had left Houston two hours before sunrise. Twenty miles farther on, the driver slowed and turned off the paved road under a rusty sign that advertised "Cabins" over an arrow and the word "Private."

"They said it was three miles off the main road," the passenger said. He had opened a box of .357 magnum cartridges and put a handful in his right coat pocket. As the driver made a sharp turn in the dirt road, they spotted the police roadblock. The Ford rolled to a stop next to several large deputies who were holding carbines. The driver spotted two more in the rearview mirror as they moved in at the rear of the Ford. The driver and passenger both rolled down their side windows. The older deputy, a sergeant, walked up to the driver. The passenger spoke: "Good morning! How y'all doing?"

The driver nodded to the older deputy. The deputy remained silent, his eyes on the driver.

"Joe Troop, FBI. We're looking for Sheriff Hayward." The passenger spoke to the younger deputy on his side of the car.

"Y'all got ID?" The older deputy asked.

"In my inside pocket," answered Daniel. Both men slowly reached with their left hands and pulled out their credentials. The deputy relaxed.

"You'll find the sheriff 'bout a mile down the road."

The driver nodded again and put the Ford into first gear.

The deputies watched the Ford drive away.

"Was that him?" The younger deputy asked as he watched the Ford drive away.

"Yep. Had to be. Didn't you see his eyes?"

"He looked smaller than I reckoned. Is it true he's part Comanche?" The younger deputy asked.

The older deputy shook his head and walked back over to his car.

As the Ford pulled into a clearing, they saw the sheriff and more of his deputies clustered around a group of vehicles to their left. On the right edge of the clearing stood a solitary figure in a white shirt and light gray Stetson. He wore a Colt model 1911 in a holster on his right hip. His gaze was focused on several small cabins that could be seen through the trees about one hundred yards in the distance.

The agents walked up behind and slightly to the man's left side.

"Mornin' Chase! State of Texas sent just one Ranger?" Daniel asked. The Ranger chuckled at the old line.

"I am glad to see that Mr. Hoover saw fit to send two of his finest. Howdy, Daniel, Joe." The men shook hands. "Let's go over and let the sheriff fill us in. Apparently, the sheriff and his boys found this bunch here late last night. His deputies have the place surrounded and there has been no movement at all."

They walked over to the other side of the clearing, and after Chase introduced the two agents, the sheriff began his briefing.

"Y'all know the details of the kidnapping in Dallas and how the gang disappeared with the kids. A source of mine called last night and told me about this bunch. They've been here for three days. She spotted one of the kids and that's when she called me. Four men showed up, but one of them left on the day they checked in and hasn't come back. We showed her photos of the kidnappers and she picked all four. So as far as we know, there's three inside with the two kids. We know the identity of the one who left on the first day and some of my boys are looking for him. The leader is an old boy from around St. Augustine. His name is Curtis and he's the one I'd worry about. The other two are Eldon Davies and Bobby Kemp, a couple of punks from Nacogdoches. They act like hard cases but they're just a couple of followers, so it's hard to say what they'll do when it comes down to the nut cuttin'."

The sheriff pulled out a large piece of paper with a diagram of the cabin drawn on it. "There's a front and back door, two bedrooms, a kitchen, and a small main room. The bedrooms are to the right as you go in the front door. I got my boys all 'round the cabin, not too close but they got a clear view of everything. We managed to get everybody else out of the other cabins. We don't know what kind of firepower they got, but you can bet that they are heavily armed. And to this minute that is all we know."

Daniel studied the diagram. "Looks like you got everything covered, Sheriff." His mind was racing ahead to his next move.

"Look, I know that kidnapping is a federal offense and I got no problem with you boys handling it. But my boys are damn good and we would sure like to be in on this."

Daniel looked up from the diagram. "I wouldn't have it any other way, Sheriff. We won't be using long guns or even a Thompson for this. So whoever goes in with us will need to be the best pistol shots you have. We've worked with Chase in the past, but we don't know any of your boys. So, if you have no objections, Chase will be with Joe and me up front and we'll do all the talking. We'll put your boys right up there with us."

The sheriff moved away from the hood of the car. "T.J., Walt! Come over here. These boys are the best shots in my office. Just tell them where you want them and what you want them to do."

Using the diagram the sheriff had laid out on the hood of his car, Daniel made his assignments and asked if anyone had questions or comments.

The sheriff was the only one who spoke. "I know all those punks in the cabin, but I know Curtis the best. He is a gutsy bastard. He is quick and not afraid to take chances. Keep a real close eye on him."

"Thanks, Sheriff. I will. Anyone else? No? Sheriff, can you get word of our plan to your boys on the perimeter? If they hear any shooting around the cabin, I want them to hold their fire until told different. Now here's how we're going to handle this."

————————

The smell of lead solvent used in the cleaning of guns permeated the wooden tabletops in the gun room. The Houston field office, like every office in the bureau, kept an arsenal of firearms secured in a large vault in the gun room. Bureau regulations decreed that any time an agent checked a weapon out of the vault, it was to be cleaned before being put back, even if it was not used.

Daniel sat with his shirt sleeves rolled neatly above the elbows, across the table from Joe Troop, who had in front of him the Thompson submachine gun. The Thompson lay in pieces, the heavy steel and brass innards placed next to the wooden stock and forestock like pieces of a jigsaw puzzle. When Troop was satisfied that everything was clean, he reassembled the weapon, and after a swipe with a cloth on the Cutts compensator to remove a smudge, he set it aside and began to clean his handgun. Daniel was equally involved with a pump shotgun and several other weapons they had checked out of the vault in the early morning hours. The special agent in charge of the division stood near the door holding a cup of coffee.

"You're sure I can't convince you to stay for our little gathering?" he asked.

"Sorry, Frank, we have trains to catch and I can't speak for Joe, but I'm not much for gatherings where the only drink is eggnog."

"Well, I appreciate you fellas hanging around to help with the press and the debriefing. I spoke to Mr. H. on the blower a few minutes ago and he asked me to pass along his appreciation. Said he was meeting with you next week, Daniel. Anything you want to tell me?"

"Just a follow-on assignment. Not sure where it'll be, but I do know it won't be in your division."

They spent a few more minutes in small talk and then the agent in charge wished them luck and went back to his office. They finished up with the weapons, put them back in the vault, and completed the required forms and other paperwork.

"What's this about a new assignment, Daniel?" Troop was washing his hands in a sink in the corner of the room.

"Sit down, Joe, and I'll bring you up to date. I think you might be interested."

Daniel walked over and closed the door and then joined Troop at the table.

"The bureau has been charged by the President to start an operation in South America. All I know for now is that it's an undercover assignment where we are to locate and identify Nazis and intercept their communications back to Germany.

The bureau has already set up operations in Mexico and the Caribbean, but I'll be with a team assigned to Uruguay. If you're interested I can get you on board."

Joe carefully folded his sleeves back down and buttoned the cuffs. He shook his head.

"Sounds real interesting, but I don't speak Spanish like you and I'd be a disaster as an undercover. Besides, I already made other plans."

"Other plans?" Daniel sat back in his chair.

"I enlisted last week. Army. I report in two days. Figured they could use a man who's pulled the trigger a few times."

"Damn, Joe, you never said a word."

"Neither did you about this business in South America," Joe smiled.

"You know that Mr. Hoover's going to be mad as hell at you?"

"Oh, I imagine he'll get over it. Besides, he'll need all the help he can get after the war and when I get back, I'll explain it all to him."

"Like hell you will," Daniel laughed. He looked at his watch. "It's about time we got down to the train depot.

Deputy Sheriff T.J. Willits stood near the door of the tourist cabin while the crime laboratory people worked inside. His hands had stopped shaking and his stomach was almost back to normal. He looked across the lot and watched as the sheriff and his captain got into their cars. Everyone else had left earlier, taking the two prisoners and the boy and girl back to town. Deputy

Willits had been left, along with two younger deputies to assist the lab people. He stood well clear of the spot where Curtis had gone down. He avoided looking at the spot and wished the lab people would hurry. He needed to get out of here. He needed a drink. After a while, the two younger deputies came around the corner of the cabin.

"How's it going, T.J.?"

"OK."

"Toby and I was talking about what happened, but we couldn't see anything because we were on the back side of the cabin. We heard one shot and that was it. What happened?"

Deputy Willits looked at both of them and shook his head.

"If you're still upset 'bout it and don't want to talk, we'll understand." The younger one said.

"Dammit! I ain't upset!" He saw the tiny smirk on their faces. "It's just that I'm still trying to figure it out. It happened so fast, it's almost like I didn't see it at all, even though I was standing right there."

"What happened so fast?" Both deputies drew closer.

"Well, the FBI fellas placed me at the corner of the cabin so's I could cover both front and side. The one they call Smoke, who, by the way, prefers to be called Daniel, took up a position about ten feet beside me and out away from the door. The other G-man, the one called Troop, was talking to Curtis and his boys through the cabin door asking them to come out so's they could talk face-to-face. In a little while, Curtis comes out of the cabin holding the girl in front of him. He has a small automatic pointed at her head and the first thing he sees is Daniel standing about ten feet in front of him. Troop and the Ranger were on the far side of the door, off to Curtis's left, and Troop was still talking to Curtis, real calm and even, almost like he's discussing the weather. All of us have our guns holstered, the G-men have their suit coats on so you can't see their pistols, and the Ranger is focused on the other two inside. Curtis is rantin' and ravin' about how he doesn't care if he dies and that he'll take the kids with him. But Troop just keeps on calm and reasonable and Daniel is standing in front of Curtis, with a little smile on his face, his hands hangin' loose at his sides. He just keeps looking at Curtis, but those eyes! If ever I seen death in someone's eyes . . . well, the calm conversation wasn't doin' any good 'cause Curtis was gettin' real antsy. He kept moving his pistol from the girl's head and pointing it at Daniel and then he'd put it back on the girl. Made me nervous as hell 'cause I thought he was going to blast Daniel, but the G-man just stood real calm with that little smile on his face. And then when Curtis started to take the gun away from the girl's head again and point it back at Daniel, it happened."

"What happened T.J.?"

"That's what I'm not sure about! The next thing I remember is seeing Daniel's pistol out in front of him and hearing that loud boom a magnum makes and Curtis is on the ground. What's botherin' me is I can't remember even seeing the G-man draw. I saw Curtis was down and Daniel had the big Smith at arm's length, his other hand pressed close to his chest, and he wasn't smiling any more. Then the little girl ran over to me, but before she got to me, I could see a hole in Curtis's forehead while he was laying on the ground. I grabbed the little girl and got her around to the side of the cabin, and the captain came and got her and took her back to where the sheriff was. Troop then starts talking to the two inside the cabin, Davies and Kemp. I guess they could see Curtis laying there in front of the door with a hole in his head and they didn't want none of that because they came out with their hands in the air. I went over and helped Daniel hook up Davies while Troop and the Ranger took Kemp. While we were putting the cuffs on Davies, Daniel leaned in and spoke in his ear. And then we got them loaded in the wagon and Daniel takes me aside and looks at me with those gray eyes and he shakes my hand and thanks me for backing him up. Can you believe that? Like he ever needed backing up!"

"Yeah. But what did he say to Davies?"

"I'm not exactly sure, but I swear I heard him say thank you."

"Why the hell would he thank a punk like Davies?"

"I don't know, but I think it was 'cause he was glad he didn't have to kill him too."

"The hell you say?" The younger deputies gave each other a skeptical look.

———— ✦ ————

The sun was down when the cab dropped the agents off on Washington Avenue in front of Houston's Grand Central Station. Joe put his suitcase down on the sidewalk.

"Guess I won't be seeing you for a while, Daniel, so good luck down there and take care of yourself around those Nazis." He held out his hand.

"Same to you, Joe. Maybe I'll see you when this war is over."

"Hope so, Daniel." They shook hands. Joe picked up his suitcase and walked into the station. Daniel, who was hungry, went inside the station to look for a café that would be open on Christmas Eve.

The cook sat on a stool at the counter watching himself blow smoke rings in the mirror behind the coffee urns. He saw Daniel walk into the café carrying a suitcase in his left hand and watched as he sat down at the far end of the counter. The cook frowned and caught the eye of the counterman, who was busy running a long thin brush down the glass tube on one of the coffee urns. The counterman looked up as Daniel sat on the stool closest to the wall. The man in the suit looked like a well-dressed businessman but there was a hardness about him that the counterman, who had served three years for petty theft, recognized. He spotted the bulge on the man's right hip that told him the man was packing. This man was either the law or one of those men they called a "shooter," the bad ones sent out to take care of business for the bosses.

"Sorry, buddy, but the kitchen is closed. I got some fresh coffee and not so fresh apple pie." He watched the man glance over at the cook and then back at him and then at the hand-written menu on the blackboard above the urns which advertised the blue plate special: Meatloaf with mashed potatoes and grilled onions.

"I'll have coffee and the pie." He smiled and slid a two-dollar bill toward the counter man. "And I'll bet that there are a couple of leftover end cuts to that meat loaf. If you'll put them between two slices of bread, I'd be obliged. Got a long way to go tonight," he pointed behind him to the inside of the station.

"They'll be cold and a little dry by now, mister." The counterman's voice softened when he looked into the man's eyes.

"Just the way I like it." The man looked over at the cook.

While the cook was preparing the sandwich, Daniel noticed three young sailors sitting at a table near the front window. They looked like they just got out of boot camp. They were engaged in a lively conversation, the brashness of youth evident in their gestures and talk, the half-empty milk shakes and cold French-fried potatoes before them on the table like so many afterthoughts lost in their excitement. He wondered which of them would live through the journey they would soon be on. He knew they would leave their confidence and brashness somewhere on the far side of the world, and that those who were lucky enough to come back from the war would never be young again. He thought about Kemp and Davies, who would probably avoid the death penalty. They would serve out their prison sentences during the war with three meals and a dry place to sleep, and would walk away years later in cheap suits with a few bucks in their pockets.

There was still another hour before his train was scheduled to leave, so Daniel took his time with the meal and thought about South America and about how each new assignment brought with it a chance to close out the old and offer up a chance for something that would hold his interest for the long term. It had been like that ever since he had come back after the last war, the one they called the Great War. When he finished his meal, he asked the counterman for the check.

"I ain't gonna charge you for stale meat loaf and pie. Not on Christmas Eve." The counterman had decided the man was probably not a "shooter." Most likely he was the law.

Daniel added another two-dollar bill to the one on the counter. He had misjudged the counterman. "This one's for you and the other is for the cook."

"Right Christian of you, mister." There was no smile from the counterman. Daniel did not expect one.

He picked up his suitcase, and as he reached the front door the counterman hollered out: "Merry Christmas, mister!"

He turned and nodded to the counterman and saw one of the young sailors look up from the table, a smile on his teenage face. Daniel closed the door, and suddenly feeling very tired, turned and walked to the trains.

Printed in the USA
CPSIA information can be obtained
at www.ICGtesting.com
LVHW091615240624
783885LV00004B/60